SWEET AS SIN

A REVERSE AGE GAP ROMANCE

SUGAR AND SCOTCH DUET BOOK TWO

D.L. DARBY

For all the women who feel stuck. It's never too late to ditch the cage and find yourself a new puppy.

CONTENTS

CONTENT WARNING

This story contains triggers such as cheating, violence, spousal violence, assault, divorce, off-page parental death, emotional abuse, mention of murder, sexually explicit scenes, foul language/profanity, and gun violence.

Please read responsibly.

and I loved you. not because of how you
made me feel but because you made me
laugh when I needed it most.

R.M. DRAKE

Sadie

Most women in my position would kill for the life I have.

A forty-seven-year-old, former model turned millionaire's wife. I get to do what I want, when I want. Invest as much money as I please in any pet projects I might have, take as many vacations as I desire, and don't even have to have dinner on the table when my husband gets home from work.

Sounds great, doesn't it?

But after almost twenty years, it takes a toll on you. You age out of the career because there is always someone younger, prettier, or cheaper to take your place. You realize your friends aren't really friends at all, just people who want to attach themselves like leeches to your good name and interminable amounts of money. You're lucky to come out on the other side of the industry with *one* good friend, let alone a group. The vacations turn sullen and solitary because you get tired of paying for everything for the so-called friends, and your husband is always too busy with work.

The same loving husband who once looked at you with nothing but adoration and pure unadulterated lust. The man who told you it would always be you who held his heart in the palm of your hand. The same hand that sported a vintage emerald cut blue diamond set in platinum. It signified the old money from which said husband hailed–and old money meant old ideals.

The plentiful vacations and romantic dinners turned into work trips that '*I wouldn't enjoy*' or were '*men-only, no wives allowed.*' But the next morning's gossip rag showed proof that while the wives weren't allowed, escorts apparently were.

"*You'll get used to it, dear. Let the men play with their toys. After all, no one said we couldn't have our fun too,*" his mother once said to me before her untimely death.

Once you get over the initial embarrassment, and learn to act like you already knew your husband stayed the night in some swanky hotel with a woman–or two–half your age, you *do* get used to it. And you find ways to cope.

My coping mechanism happened to be food and sun. So, I bought myself a condo right on the beach in sunny Jacksonville, Florida. The bright cream walls and soft blue accents were my home away from my other home in the concrete jungle that was New York City.

On my first night in Jacksonville, I took myself to dinner at a cute little waterfront restaurant with a patio lit up with torches and framed with low bushes of the best smelling azaleas.

When you're a model, they don't let you eat cake. Or at least they didn't when I was one. Cake is my coping method. Especially cupcakes, because they are compact and cute. You can make them into little sandwiches and stuff them entirely in your mouth on a particularly bad day when your phone is blowing up with the latest gossip about what–or who–your husband has been doing while you're out of town.

When I tell you this restaurant had the best damn cake I've ever had in my life, I mean every single word of praise for the delightful confections. They had these things from a pop-up bakery called Caketails. Little shot glasses full of cake, cream, and fruit that came in multiple different flavors that just exploded in your mouth.

Caketails were worth investing money in—something to keep me busy and away from New York. So, of course, I hunted down the woman who made them and forced her to become my friend and give me all her secret recipes.

She didn't give me her recipes, but she did become the first genuine friend I'd had in a long, long time. Together, we achieved her dream of opening a bakery/café that turned into a small plates/bar in the evening.

Sugar and Scotch, we called it.

That was three years ago, and the place quickly became a huge success. I took care of the business portion of it–thanks to taking online classes and receiving a business degree the moment I realized my modeling career was coming to an end in my mid-thirties. And she, Rylee, took care of all the rest.

We make a good team. It was us against the world; the sky was the limit. But then she started dating her much younger boyfriend, Chance–and with Chance came his best friend, Tyler, who was also in his mid-twenties.

With Tyler came the memory of my mother-in-law's words to me years before. *'No one said we couldn't have our fun too.'*

But Tyler was the dangerous kind of fun. The kind that looks at you like you hold up the sun and the moon, and he wants to drop to his knees and worship between your legs because he thinks you're a goddess. The kind that drinks down every last drop and then fills you up again so he can start over. That ruins you for any other man. That brands himself on your soul.

Tyler was the kind of fun you didn't want to give up. So I didn't want to indulge...even a little.

But *fuck* if the persistent bastard wasn't like a custard-filled golden cupcake that I wanted to stuff in my mouth every single time I saw him.

CHAPTER ONE

"Does it feel tight?"

"Yeah."

"Okay, squeeze it a little, and then go slow."

"It feels better if I go faster."

"Slow down! It's messy when you go fast."

"So bossy. That's fine. More for me to lick up later."

"You like it when I'm bossy. Your movements are awkward. Doesn't that feel funny?"

"No. It feels just fine to me. I may not be as good at this as you are, but my results are undeniably delicious."

"And undeniably ugly," Rylee said, swiping a finger through the bright pink frosting on the cupcake I was piping.

"Hey! I worked hard on that!" I cried and batted her hand away.

"Worked hard at making a mess so you can eat all

the unsellable treats." She laughed as she broke a chunk of the small confection off and popped it into her mouth.

I grabbed one as well, the chocolate cake giving easily as I tore it in half, squeezed some raspberry buttercream on it, and mashed the halves together before stuffing it in my mouth.

She raised an eyebrow at my squirrel cheeks and swallowed her bite. "Do you wanna talk about it?"

"Talk about what?" I muttered with my mouth full, my words barely discernible.

Rylee's eyes flitted to the iPad on the table, where the bright screen glowed with a photo of my husband leaving a restaurant—his hand on the lower back of some petite, pretty brunette.

The headline on the article read, '*Scott Tailor steps out with another woman?*' With a byline of, '*Wife of multi-millionaire hasn't been seen in the city in weeks. Trouble in paradise?*'

Wife of....

They hadn't even bothered to use my name until the actual article. I'd been reduced to '*the scorned wife of*' and '*former model and trophy wife of.*' More and more gossip columns had been popping up lately —a new one for every summons from my *dear* husband that I ignored.

"I don't understand why you put up with it, Sadie. Why don't you just leave him?" Rylee asked as she reached over and shut the keyboard case that the iPad rested in.

The din from the bakery bar we owned filtered through the double doors leading from the bar to the kitchen where we currently were. It was lunchtime, and the afternoon rush that came in to grab sandwiches, soups, and sweet treats to give them a sugar boost to get through the rest of their workdays, was in full swing.

It was a sound that made me happy. To know that Rylee and I had created a space people enjoyed occupying during their break from their humdrum jobs. To know we supplied them with freedom, if only for a little while, and put smiles on their faces.

None of it would have been possible without the money I'd invested in it.

So, I gave my best friend a tight smile and answered, "You know I like the comfort of my life, Ry. If I tried to leave him, he'd make my life miserable. He'd take the condo, and you know he'd try to take this place."

"We're doing just fine. We can take out a loan to pay back the money of his that you invested into it. And aren't you entitled to alimony? It's not like he could try and fight you if you filed and said it was because he's cheating. It's splashed all over the New York gossip columns every week!"

I snorted. "He's Scott Tailor. He'd probably be able to convince a judge it was *me* who was cheating on *him,* so what other choice did he have but to find comfort in the bosom of all the pretty young things he parades around the city?"

A pair of midnight eyes flashed in my mind for a moment. The gentle touch of soft lips against mine. The smell of cedar and sweet mint. A rich, breathy tenor whispering, *"It can be our little secret."*

"So fucking stupid. I hate this for you," Rylee murmured as she started piping cupcakes the way they were meant to be piped.

I didn't respond, lost in my thoughts. I don't know how much time passed, with me staring at nothing and her working on bakery items, before she gently cleared her throat.

"Anything new on the Tyler front?"

Tyler Michaelson. Best friend of her boyfriend, Chance. Both skirted twenty years our junior and were—*are*—relentless in their pursuit. Chance and Rylee had been dating for nearly six months, but it had been a long, twisted road of *Jerry Springer* bullshit before their relationship finally settled and secured.

Long story short, Chance was the son of Rylee's former high school boyfriend, who broke her heart when he got Chance's mother pregnant. No, Chance hadn't known who Rylee was—and vice versa—when they met. Yes, Rylee was utterly mortified when she found out. No, neither she, Chance, nor Devon—Chance's dad—took it well.

But yes, love prevailed, and six months after the boys walked into the bar, here we are. He's going to propose soon, and she has no idea. I know she'll say yes.

During all this, Chance's best friend Tyler had been doing everything in his power to woo me. From the second he walked into the bar to grab Chance away from flirting with Rylee, the moment we laid eyes on each other, he'd been calling me his future wife.

He was tall, tanned, dark-haired, and treated me like a goddess—everything I love in a man. And at first, I was annoyed. I'm married, and Tyler was a temptation being dangled in front of my face like a cat with a mouse on a string.

But he'd become a friend over the last few months. Someone to talk to and confide in. Since Rylee spent the majority of her time with Chance now, I'd found myself quite lonely; and as if he knew that what I really needed was a shoulder to lean on, Tyler had really been there for me.

He was wild and carefree. But with me, he could be profound and insightful. And I sometimes found myself daydreaming about what it would be like to leave my husband and dive headfirst into the world of the twenty-six-year-old.

But I was a creature of comfort. Nearly twenty years in my multiple lavish homes and the ability to do whatever I wanted whenever I wanted didn't have me running toward a life of struggle and working myself to death.

Sure, the bar was popular, and we were financially okay, but I'd have to work seven days a week, open to close, just to afford the dues on my one-point-two-million-dollar condo on the beach.

Tyler owned half of a landscaping company, with Chance owning the other half. And while they were doing just fine with their business, even combining our incomes wouldn't allow me to live the life I liked.

Yet, sometimes I wanted to think about it. To let those little whispers of secrets and the passing soft touches get under my skin.

But I shouldn't have even been entertaining thoughts of that nature.

Because I wasn't my husband. Why be married if you were just going to cheat all the time? If he had been anyone else, I would have left him, but I'd been content to let him do his thing while I did mine and spent his money.

Let him make an ass out of himself.

"Tyler and I are just friends, Ry. You know that." I gathered my things. I didn't want to have this conversation again, and I had errands to run before needing to be back for the bar shift later in the evening.

"One day, he's going to wear you down," she sang, her attention not leaving the cake she was now decorating. I didn't answer, and her soft laughter followed me as I went out the back of the kitchen.

She didn't deserve my attitude. I was only irritated because I knew there was truth to her statement.

A fucking dildo only did the job so many times before you wanted the real thing. And after weeks of my husband being photographed with various young women, I sure as fuck wasn't going back to New York to sit on his dick.

CHAPTER TWO

Tyler

BEING SICK SUCKED.

I rarely got sick enough to bail on Chance for work, but I felt like I'd been hit by a truck. An inferno roared beneath my skin, but my body shivered as though I'd just taken one of the many ice-cold showers that had become part of my daily routine whenever I was in close proximity to Sadie.

My head pounded. The aching throb that had settled between my temples sometime in the early morning, continued its beat throughout the entire day, and nothing I had taken would make it stop. I was tired and hungry and had no desire to leave the comfort of my king-sized bed. On days like this, I wished my sister lived closer. Or that I had more friends.

Chance was pretty much my only friend–well, I suppose I could count Rylee in that circle now, too. And Sadie...well, I didn't know what she was. Did I want to consider her a friend? No. I wanted to consider her full of my cock every waking moment of every day.

The last few weeks had been agony. Every single time her fucking husband stepped out on her, she'd come running to me.

It was pure torture for us both.

Ever since that night at Sugar and Scotch two months ago, when our relationship finally showed its true colors, and she had dropped the pretense of not wanting me, something changed between us. We both knew it. We both wanted to act on it, but she wouldn't do it again. Not after Rylee walked in on us just as my lips touched Sadie's.

When my words had finally made it through that beautiful brain of hers and convinced her she could be happy, too.

That no one had to know.

That we could keep it a secret.

The sound of the doorbell cut through my delirious daydreams of what could have been that night. It was like an arrow piercing me straight through the temples, and I groaned, mumbling for whoever it was to go away before I realized they wouldn't have been able to hear me. I didn't move as I thought about who it could be at the door. Chance knew I was sick, so it was possible it was him with soup and more medicine. He did say he'd be by to check on me later or that if work got too busy, he'd send Rylee.

I didn't even know what time it was.

Mustering the energy to haul myself up, my breath caught in the back of my throat, causing a dry cough to send me into a series of nasty-sounding hacks. The doorbell dinged again as I grabbed my knockoff Teenage Mutant Ninja Turtle Snuggie my sister made me from its place on the back of the over-sized black leather chair in the corner of my room. I pulled it over my head as I trudged down the hall to the door, flipping the Donatello hood up as I yanked the door open just as the doorbell went off for the third time.

"I swear to God, if you ring that doorbell again, I'm going to–" I cut myself off as I peered out from beneath the hood and took in the shoes on my doorstep. Sadie's favorite Valentino black braided espadrilles stared back at me, and I quickly flipped my hood back and looked up at the woman who ran rampant in my mind all day. She looked radiant in a simple plum-colored wrap dress and scrutinized me with a raised brow.

Straightening up, I leaned against the doorframe, crossing my arms as I did my best to temper my surprise. I certainly hadn't been expecting to see her today. I nodded in greeting and tried to sound suave as I asked, "What's up, Wifey?"

The words died with another hoarse cough I attempted to keep inside my chest. My headache flared, and sweat started to drip down my back under the heaviness of my hooded blanket.

"Should I start calling you dude instead of Pup?" she asked mischievously.

Under normal circumstances, her impish tone would have had me standing at attention. However, all my playfulness was nowhere to be found as I doubled over and succumbed to my coughing fit.

"Come on now, little turtle. Let's get you back into bed," she said in the most soothing tone I had ever heard from her.

"Don't act like you're my mom," I managed between wheezes. Pulling the Snuggie over my head, I flung it away, my body temperature rising as my coughing continued. "You're gonna get sick. Why are you here?"

"Hey," she said sharply as she walked toward the kitchen to set down the grocery bags I hadn't noticed before. "I'm not a caregiver by nature, so be happy I'm even over here. Also, I'm immune to whatever crap you've got. I don't even remember the last time I was sick. My housekeeper in New York, Claudia, makes me these elderberry shots I take every morning. She overnights them every two weeks unless I'm scheduled to return."

She held up one of the bags and motioned to it, and I was taken aback at her thoughtfulness. "You came over here to make me a health shot?" I fell onto the couch and threw my arm over my eyes. I was sticky, and my sweatpants had dark gray spots where my sweat was seeping through.

"No, I brought you some of mine. She said they

also help when you're already sick. So, why don't you take this and then go take a cold shower?" Her voice sounded closer now, and I peeked out from behind my arm to see her standing over me with a glass of something purple and lumpy.

I looked at it skeptically. "Why are you being nice to me?"

"I'm always nice to you, Pup." Sadie placed the drink on the glass coffee table in front of the couch, on a coaster from a set she brought over from her house a few game nights ago. She keeps saying she forgets it, but I feel like she left them because she absolutely hates when people don't use coasters. It's just one of her many quirks I have filed away under 'nonsense about Sadie I might need to use one day.'

I shamelessly watched her hips swinging side to side as she walked back into my kitchen, her perfectly round ass just begging for me to follow and grab it. Instead, I reached over and grabbed the glass with the lumpy, purple mixture that was still half-frozen and gulped it down.

It actually tasted good, like a berry smoothie with a hint of mint and a slight, sharp undertone of ginger. The coolness from the drink slid down my throat and eased the ache all my coughing had caused. When it was gone, I raised the empty glass to my forehead and laid back, my eyes never leaving Sadie as she zipped around my kitchen, humming something I couldn't place.

I'd never seen her so...domestic.

I fucking loved it.

If only I felt better to be able to enjoy it.

"What are you doing in there, Wifey?" I croaked, my throat tender.

"Heating some vegetable soup that Claudia makes for Scott when he's under the weather."

I grimaced and placed the glass back on the coaster before jackknifing into a seated position. "Don't say his name in my house," I snapped as I stood.

Sadie paused, and her gaze lifted from the stove to focus on the cabinet at her eye level. I watched as she shifted slightly, and my cock stirred in my sweats, despite the shitty way I felt. I knew what that tone of voice did to her. It was the same one I'd used that night at the bakery–the one that had finally crumbled those walls she built so high around her heart.

She finally looked over at me, and I could tell by her demeanor she was sorry. But she wouldn't say it. I knew the words would never leave those luscious lips. The thought of walking into the kitchen and bending her over the counter consumed me as my temples started to throb again.

Her eyes moved down my body slowly, over my naked chest, until they settled on the outline of my cock. She swallowed visibly before she turned her attention back to the soup. "You should go take that shower since you're all sweaty," she said unevenly.

I almost took a step toward her when another cough erupted from my throat, so I turned away quickly and headed back to my room. I left my door open, and the door to my en-suite bathroom, and turned the walk-in shower on high pressure with the coolest temperature I could stand.

The water felt great on my skin, but it caused that weird itchy feeling in the hollow of my throat. By the time I lazily washed the sweat from my body, my teeth chattered, and there were goosebumps along my skin. The inferno that had consumed me for the better part of the day was temporarily quelled, but the cough seemed to persist.

I didn't bother getting dressed again as I walked back out to the kitchen with only a fluffy white towel wrapped around my waist. Sadie didn't look up from where she was perched at the end of my couch, glaring at her phone with an aggravated look. Her lips were turned down, and I had a hunch her husband was to blame.

The soup she'd warmed up was gently simmering in the pot, and a ladle sat in the spoon rest next to the stove. Dipping the ladle in the steaming liquid, I lifted it to my nose to inhale the savory scent of roasted vegetables and garlic. It was viscous, like the vegetables had been roasted then put through a blender. The flavors exploded on my tongue as they warmed and eased the itch in my throat. I expected it to be salty from how it smelled, but the broth was natural and garlicky with a hint of cinnamon.

I slurped down two ladlefuls before my stomach felt full, then noticed a Vitaminwater in the dragonfruit flavor I liked, sitting on the kitchen island. It seemed as though Sadie had been paying attention to me all these months, more than she wanted to let on.

My body felt sluggish, and I wanted nothing more than to crawl back into my bed, but the fact that Sadie was still here couldn't be ignored–even if she was still ignoring me. I flipped the switch on the burner to turn the soup off and unscrewed the cap from the Vitaminwater to take a large gulp before placing it in the fridge so it could get cold. I don't care what anyone says. None of those flavors are good unless they are cold or over ice.

"You should get back to bed. Feel any better after your shower?" Sadie asked. If she'd pulled her attention away from her phone when I was slurping soup, I wouldn't have known, but she didn't look at me as I stalked toward her in nothing but my towel.

Grabbing her phone out of her hands, I tossed it on the matching loveseat, holding back a laugh when she sputtered as she tried to reach for it. When she stopped and glared up at me, she finally realized I was in nothing but a towel, and my dick was mere inches away from her face.

"That was rude," she huffed and very carefully leaned back as she crossed her arms, making sure not to break eye contact with me.

I cursed whatever higher power there was that I was sick instead of being able to use our situation to further try to get her to succumb to me. But I grinned down at her before walking around the coffee table to the other end of the couch. "Why did you stay if you're just going to be on your phone the whole time?"

Sitting in the middle of the couch, I kicked up my legs and positioned myself to lie back in her lap. My head hit her thigh just as she reached for her phone, and she let out a startled yelp as the water from my hair seeped through her dress.

"Tyler! What do you think you're doing?" she shouted as she raised her hands to avoid touching me.

"Play with my hair? Pleeaaassse?" I smiled widely up at her while scooting back so that my head rested in the dip between her legs.

She blinked, looking down at me like I was a wild animal that would attack her if she moved a muscle. "Pup, you just got me soaked, and now I'm going to have to go home and change before going back to the bar tonight."

I waggled my eyebrows at her. "Not the first time I made you soaking wet, is it?"

Her eyebrows relaxed as she dropped her hands to my head, and a smile stretched across her face. "Yeah, I walked into that one, didn't I? You *must* be feeling better."

She began to play with my hair absentmindedly, and it wasn't long before I felt myself drifting closer to sleep as her nails lightly scratched against my scalp. "Sadie?"

"Yeah, Pup?"

My eyes closed and my head fell to the side, my cheek resting against her thigh as I mumbled, "Thank you for taking care of me. I feel better now that you're here."

I hoped my tone conveyed that I was being serious. Humor was often my shield for how I really felt most of the time, but I wanted her to know that I was genuinely thankful she was there and had brought things to help me get better. Raising my left hand, I rested it in the space between her and the couch and flattened my palm against her lower back.

Words couldn't really express how I felt at that moment. As her fingers passed through my hair, I felt the tension of being so close to me evaporate from her body. If only she'd say *'fuck you'* to her cheating husband, this could be an everyday occurrence for us.

"Hey, Pup?"

"Yeah, Wifey?"

"Your towel came undone."

CHAPTER THREE

"TELL ME YOU SAW HIS DICK. PLEASE, PLEASE, *please*, tell me you saw it. I have been waiting for this moment for months now," Rylee babbled, trying to get me to look at her from where she was standing in the doorway of our office at Sugar and Scotch.

"To see Tyler's dick? My, my, my, what would Chance say?" I replied, looking at her sideways as I smirked before focusing my attention back on the computer as I worked on the books for the month.

"Sadie, shut it and tell me right now. Did. You. See. Tyler's. Dick?"

"Yes! Are you happy now? I saw Tyler's dick in all its impressive glory. Even flaccid, it was remarkable. Did I go home afterward and use my shower head while I thought about it? Abso-fucking-lutley I did, and I am not ashamed of it." I slapped my pen down on the desk and spun the chair around.

To see Tyler standing just behind Rylee with a huge fucking smile.

"You dirty bitch! Oh my God, this makes me so excited! Is that weird that I'm excited that you're finally giving in to your attraction to him?" Rylee chattered on, clearly unaware he was standing right behind her.

I felt my cheeks redden, and the flush crept down my neck and over my chest. There was no way he hadn't heard my confession, and I bit the inside of my cheek while internally cursing myself for admitting what I'd done.

"I'm all for it," he remarked.

Rylee yelped and twirled around, holding a hand to her chest before she smacked him lightly on the shoulder. "You fucking scared me. I didn't even hear you come in. What are you doing... Oh, fuck. You totally just heard that, didn't you?"

"I sure did." His tone dropped lower as he continued to look at me. He looked a lot better than he had the other day, and I assumed he was feeling better if he was here. But *why* he was here, I hadn't a clue.

Rylee looked over her shoulder at me, and I flashed her a look, silently begging her not to leave me alone with him. Of course, like the amazing friend she is, she ignored me. "I'm just gonna be in the kitchen decorating cupcakes."

She disappeared, and I spun back around as Tyler walked into the room and closed the door behind him. "You can leave that open, Pup. You look like you're feeling better."

I picked my pen up and started going back through the receipts, flipping through the papers as I punched numbers into the small calculator on my right.

Tyler ignored my comment, and I heard him saunter across the room until his hands appeared on either side of me as he gripped the arms of the chair I was sitting in. The hairs on my forearms stood up, and I stopped punching the buttons as my skin broke out in goosebumps at the feeling of his warm breath on the back of my neck.

"I'm feeling much better, thanks to my nurse," he murmured. I felt him nuzzle the back of my hair before his lips ghosted the shell of my ear. "Especially now that I know she went home and came to the thought of my cock."

Letting out a breath, I closed my eyes. That incredible ache filled my lower belly and flowed between my legs. I shifted, pressing my thighs together, and I heard Tyler chuckle softly. One of his hands dropped from the arm of the chair to rest close to my bare knee, the skirt of my black sheath dress bunched on my upper thighs from the position I sat in.

"Do you know how hard that makes me, Sadie? To know that you went home and pleasured yourself and thought about me while you did it. Do you do that often? Think of me between your legs while you make yourself come?"

His fingers lightly trailed along my naked thigh. He drifted them slowly, closer to the crease between my legs. Higher, in search of that sensitive area that burned with desire at the thought of what those fingers could do to me.

"Tell me," he whispered roughly. He dropped his head lower and the scruff of his facial hair scraped against my cheek.

I clenched my thighs tighter as his hand finally moved between them, mere inches away from where I really wanted them. It couldn't travel further with how hard I squeezed, so he grabbed the skin on the inside of my thigh instead.

A low whimper left my lips, and I heard his breath hitch. All I wanted was to open my legs wide and let him touch me. Consequences be damned. I was soaked, and horny. My chest heaved with labored breaths and my hands twitched from where they were firmly planted on the desk. I wanted to reach up and grab the back of his neck and turn my head to find his lips with my own.

But I couldn't.

The glare of the diamond on my finger scowled up at me as I opened my eyes, reminding me I shouldn't be in the position I currently found myself in. I felt like I'd been doused with a bucket of cold water and pushed Tyler's hand away. He sighed against my ear before pressing a chaste kiss to my hair.

"I'm never going to stop trying," he stated. He pushed off the chair and backed up as I stood, turning to face him.

"Tyler–"

"I know. I know." He raised his hands in defeat and then shoved them into the pockets of his zip-up hoodie. "I just dropped by to give you this."

He pulled a small envelope out of his pocket and held it out for me to take. "It's just a little something to say thank you for taking care of me the other day."

"You didn't have to get me anything, Tyler. It's what friends do," I replied, but took the envelope anyway. It was sea-foam green, and the name of my favorite spa in town was scrawled across the front in elegant white script. I popped the seal on it and peeked inside to see the unmistakable shiny plastic of a gift card.

"Tyler, this was unnecessary. But thank you."

"I wanted to show you my appreciation. Since you won't let me show you the way I want to." He grinned and waggled his eyebrows at me.

Rolling my eyes, I laughed as he turned and opened the door. "Game night this weekend?" he asked.

A crushing weight settled on my shoulders as I looked down and answered, "I have to go to New York this weekend."

The room instantly felt smaller, like all the air

had been sucked from it. My lungs felt tight as I raised my eyes to see that his had hardened while he clenched his jaw. He gave me a simple nod, and I found myself scrambling to say something, *anything*, to ease the tension.

"Scott won't be there. He's out of town on business. There are some matters I need to take care of with a fundraiser our foundation has coming up."

His tone was soft as he declared, "You don't have to explain yourself to me, Sadie."

Giving him a small smile, I held up the gift card in my hands. "Thanks again. I'll see you when I get back?"

He opened the door, flipped his hood up, and raised his hand in farewell. "You know it. Have a good trip, Wifey."

CHAPTER FOUR

Tyler

Scott *fucking* Tailor.

I didn't think I could ever hate someone as much as I hated that prick. The man had to be a real piece of shit to publicly parade various women through the city while married. He'd embarrassed Sadie numerous times since I'd known her, and he'd been doing it for a lot longer than that.

Rylee was always asking Sadie why she didn't just file for divorce. Neither she nor Chance understood Sadie's hesitancy.

But I did.

For some reason, besides the fact that she was fucking perfect, Scott didn't want to let Sadie go. He was like a kid acting out for attention. Always calling and texting her, and when she ignored him, he pouted and then made headlines with some leggy blonde, brunette, or redhead.

His personal affairs were just as dirty as his business practices. A fucking millionaire because he bought up smaller companies and sold them off in parts for profit, just like his father before him. The Tailors were old money, brought up and raised on others' misfortune.

Men like Scott got what they wanted, when they wanted it, and no one questioned them. And Scott didn't want to lose Sadie–if only to say he *had* her.

It made me sick.

The thought of Sadie returning to New York every few weeks to see him drove me fucking crazy. Even if she said he was gone when she was there, sometimes I wondered if she was telling me the truth. She had no reason to lie, but it seemed as though she always wanted to reassure me.

And that's precisely why I wouldn't stop trying to get her to give in to her attraction to me.

Sadie deserved to be happy. I could make her happy. I *wanted* to make her happy. I wanted to worship between her legs every moment of every day. I'd never desired a woman as badly as I desired her.

From the moment I saw her, I knew she would either break my heart or make me the happiest man alive. Finding out *who* she was hadn't changed anything. Even if she *was* the wife of the man who–

"Tyler! Earth to Tyler!" Chance's voice rang out right next to my ear.

I jolted from my reverie and reached up to take out one of my AirPods. "Just Pretend" by Bad Omens was still playing as I turned to see Chance standing in the middle of my home gym. "What's up, buddy?"

"Dude, I called you and rang your doorbell a million times before letting myself in. I saw your truck in the driveway and figured you were in here listening to music," he said as he moved between my free weights and over to the power rack to sit on the bench. "What's got you all spacey?"

A ding sounded in the ear that still had an AirPod in it, and I glanced down at my phone to see I had a text from Sadie.

> Just landed. I swear it takes me all weekend to shower off the stench of this city.

I grinned, a sinful thought filling my head of her in the shower, dripping wet, while she pleasured herself with the shower head to the thought of my cock.

"Never mind. There's only one woman who causes you to make those stupid faces at your phone. You look like a schoolgirl who just got a text from her crush," Chance joked.

I looked up to see him grinning at me. He was the only one, besides Sadie, that I told everything—well, not *everything*—to. He knew I was wearing her down, just like Rylee knew. And regardless of her being married, they were both in full support of my efforts.

"The captain of the football team only makes sense for the head cheerleader," I quipped as I stood to take my weights off the rack.

"Who's the football player, and who's the cheerleader in this situation?" Chance asked as he stood to help me.

Looking over my shoulder at him, I smirked. "It could go either way."

My phone buzzed, signaling an incoming call, as I set the weights back on their rack. I saw Chance grab my phone from my peripheral and watched a smile spread over his face as he hit accept and put the call on speakerphone.

"What's up, trouble?" he greeted.

I heard a familiar melodic voice laugh as the woman on the other end of the line gave Chance her own greeting. "What's up with you, fucker? I heard you're about to propose to Rylee! And I realized that I haven't been down to meet this woman who has swept you off your feet and turned you to mush. So I was thinking of taking the weekend off to visit. Daphne is about to leave for her honeymoon and said if I wanted to go, now was the time to do it, so we aren't both gone at the same time."

"Hell yeah! Rylee has been wanting to meet you. Get your ass on a plane." Chance looked at me and continued, "Sadie is gone all weekend, so that sucks you won't get to meet her."

I shook my head and motioned with my hands in a silent signal for him to shut up. He furrowed his fucking brows at me and shook his head with an expression of *'what's your problem'* pasted on his face.

"Who's Sadie? Wait, she's Rylee's friend, right? Married, lives in New York half the time?"

Chance threw me a dirty look as he made a motion to zip his lips, which signaled he'd let me handle this one.

Couldn't have shut your mouth earlier, dude?

I sighed. "Yeah, she's her best friend. You'll just have to meet her another time. It's no big deal. You got a ticket already?"

"Yep, figured you wouldn't care if I crashed in the guest room. Bout to board a plane in two hours. Talk to you soon!"

"Alright, call when you land. Can't wait to see you," I replied before ending the call.

"What was that about? Have you not told her about Sadie?" Chance asked.

"Why would I tell her about Sadie?"

"Why would you keep it from her? It's been months, Ty."

"She doesn't need to know about every part of my life, Chance. Besides, there's nothing to tell." My tone was absolute, leaving no room to continue the conversation.

He gave me a weird look, scrutinizing me like he was seeing a side he hadn't seen before. In all the years we'd been friends, we'd never gotten into so much as a disagreement. Even when Sadie and I had conspired against him and Rylee in an attempt to get them back together, and it had blown up in his face. Granted, they had been fine a few days later, but still, we'd never been mad at each other.

But as I said, I didn't tell Chance *everything* that went on in my life. There were things the people I cared most about in Jacksonville still didn't know about me, and I planned to keep it that way for as long as I could.

CHANCE HAD DROPPED the conversation and invited me over to his and Rylee's for dinner, before I needed to go to the airport. Not that I wanted to lose my business partner, but Chance could be a professional chef if he wanted to. I never missed an opportunity to eat a home-cooked meal at their house. Rylee had even made us a batch of peanut butter oatmeal cookies, even if she thought cookies were the worst dessert ever.

I left their house after helping them clean up. Domino even let me give him head scratches on my way out the door. The moody cat couldn't decide whether he liked me or not, and I suspected it was because he sensed I was more of a dog person.

Once I'd picked up my surprise visitor and got her settled in, I jumped in the shower to wash the day away. The hot water scalded my skin, but I relished the bite of the spray. The pain combined with the pleasure as thoughts of Sadie in the shower filled my head again. The imagery caused my cock to harden, and I gripped myself with a soapy hand, letting out a low moan that echoed against the glass-tiled walls of my walk-in shower.

I still hadn't responded to her text from earlier, and in a split decision, opened the door and grabbed my phone off the vanity. Flipping the camera open, I angled it down to snap a photo of my soaped-up cock that stood at full attention, and sent it to Sadie without hesitation.

> For all those showers you'll be taking to wash New York away. Don't wear out your shower head. The real thing is waiting for you when you get back home.

Not waiting for her response, I set my phone back on the vanity before stepping back into the shower. I wrapped my hand around my dick and started to pump it, leaning my other hand against the wall. I was larger than most guys, and my size had always been an issue with past girlfriends. Nearly nine inches erect, and my fingertips barely touched as they wrapped around my shaft.

I thought about the look on Sadie's face when I peeked up at her after she told me my towel had come undone. How she licked her lips before bolting off the couch, letting my head thump against the cushion, leaving me to leisurely secure my towel around my waist again. I visualized her taking my size with no problem, eager to sink onto my dick and ride me to completion.

Gripping harder, I stroked myself in long quick motions as I closed my eyes and thought about her rushing home to seek pleasure as she thought of me. I visualized her sinking to her knees and begging for a taste of my cock. I thought of laying her out on my bed as she took me down her throat greedily, milking me with those sweet, luscious lips of hers.

The breathy little moan that had escaped those lips when I was touching her in her office resonated in my ears, causing me to come with a loud grunt. Thick ropes of my cum painted the wall of my shower as I replayed that moan again and again in my head until I was spent.

When I was finished with my shower, I quickly checked my phone, only to be hit with the disappointment of an empty screen and no sign that Sadie had even received my message. She usually responded right away, even when she was in New York.

Sleep had trouble finding me as I tossed and turned, thinking about her there and the possibility that she'd gone running home to her husband to avoid me. I didn't want to think of the probability of that being the case. Or that it would crush me if she allowed her cheating husband to touch her, but she wouldn't let me worship her like she deserved.

In the morning, when I woke up, Sadie still hadn't texted back. And my heart sank just a little at the prospect of me being right in my assumptions.

Scott was in New York.

CHAPTER FIVE

AN ORIGINAL JACKSON POLLOCK WAS THE FIRST thing that greeted me when I opened my eyes Saturday morning. A jarring reminder that I was not in my beachside condo in Jacksonville. Groaning, I burrowed into my king-sized goose-down pillows, the silver silk of my bed sheets sliding against my skin.

I lifted my arms over my head and stretched. My midnight blue nightgown rode up my thighs as my toes tangled in the duvet that I'd kicked to the end of the California King in a giant heap of bunched silk.

Luxurious. Everything in this penthouse was luxurious. It was a life I cherished while in the city, but was happy to leave behind when I returned to the place I now thought of as home.

My slippers were waiting on the side of the bed, and the matching robe to my nightgown was draped on the back of the dove-gray velvet chaise in my corner of the room. I quickly put them on and headed to the kitchen, where I could smell my favorite brand and blend of coffee—Blue Mountain Panama Catuai—being freshly brewed.

After pouring a cup, I settled by a large corner window to look out at the East River, while savoring my first sip as the steam caressed my face. The sun had barely begun its ascent, the air too crisp to enjoy the sunrise on the terrace.

After I'd made it home from the airport the night before, I'd showered, put on my best Louboutins and a classic little black dress, and taken myself to an early dinner. It had been quiet and relaxing until I realized my people-watching had gone on too long, and the paparazzi had caught wind of where I was.

I'd smiled politely and answered a few questions on the short walk to my town car. Scott and I used to take a limo everywhere, but I'd opted for something a little more discreet for dinner.

You can take the girl out of New York, but you can't take New York out of the girl, at least not entirely, anyway.

And just like I did every time I came home and had the penthouse to myself, I plugged my phone in next to my purse in the foyer and went to bed early after a long soak in a bath full of bubbles.

Lifting my cup for another sip, I grabbed my phone in the other hand and disconnected the cord with my fingers. There were a few texts from Rylee and a missed call from Claudia, who was out at breakfast with her sister before she went to the market to get fresh flowers and fruit like she usually did on Saturday mornings. She had also texted me, but when I went to check it, I noticed a message from Tyler that had come in after I'd gone to bed.

Opening it, I gasped. "Holy fuck!"

My thighs tensed as arousal shot through me at the sight of his ridiculously exceptional penis staring back at me. I read the message that came with it and let out a giggle, one that only came about where Tyler was concerned.

"In all our years together, I don't think I've ever heard you make that sound."

The sharp tenor cut through the quiet and caused me to jump, coffee nearly spilling over the rim of my mug as I spun around to see an all too familiar pair of dark umber eyes staring back at me.

His hands were tucked in the pockets of his deep navy Tom Ford suit pants, his jacket unbuttoned over a crisp white dress shirt. His light brown hair was perfectly coiffed and looked a little longer than the last time I had seen him, and he was freshly shaven. My body clenched in places I wished it wouldn't when it came to him. After all he'd done, its reaction to him was a betrayal to me.

"What's got you in such a good mood this morning, Mrs. Tailor?"

I blacked out the screen on my phone discreetly and regained my composure. Lifting my head, I narrowed my eyes and raised a perfectly manicured eyebrow, appraising him from head to toe and back again. "Certainly not the current view, that's for sure. I thought you would be gone this weekend, *Mr. Tailor.*"

Scott smirked and prowled closer. His steps were slow as his eyes ran down my body, hands still in his pockets as he stopped before me. His eyes settled on mine, the gaze of a predator about to tear apart its prey. I'd seen men crumble under that look.

But I wasn't a man.

"What were you giggling at, Sadie?" he asked. His tone was quieter now that he was closer, but still held that edge of authority to it. It had never worked on me before, and I wondered why he thought it would be any different now.

In fact, I had half a mind to open my phone and show him exactly what had caused me to make the sound that was so foreign to his ears. "Last time I checked, Scott, you weren't my father. So keep your nose out of my business. Why are you here?"

His jaw clenched, and his eyes narrowed. I wanted him to know he didn't intimidate me, so I turned and walked back into the kitchen to fill my mug with more coffee, slipping my phone into the pocket of my robe.

"I may not be your father, but I can still lock you up and take away your privileges, or have you forgotten?" he asked jokingly.

I didn't find it funny.

His steps echoed mine as he followed me—slow and calculated, and seconds after I returned the coffee pot to its home on the Calacatta marble countertop, I could feel Scott at my back. His hands came around to rest on the counter on either side of me. Turning slowly, I raised my mug to take a sip before sweetly shooting back, "That might work on all the whores you bring back here, but you don't want to make your lovely wife unhappy, do you, dear husband? After all, a happy wife *is* a happy life, right? A caged animal will eventually ruin you once you let it out again."

The playfulness seeped from his eyes immediately, and he straightened. "I don't bring anyone here, Sadie."

"Right. You take them to the apartment at Bryant Park. Forgive me for getting my facts wrong. There's something different printed in the papers daily," I deadpanned.

"Knock it off, Sadie. Like you don't have someone in Jacksonville," he spat as he finally stepped back and out of my personal space.

My eyes widened a fraction at his accusation, and I did my best to temper down the look that crossed my face as I thought of Tyler for a split second. But that split second was all it took for Scott to look like I'd just told him I'd lost all of our money gambling at the roulette table in Vegas.

His head cocked as his hands clenched into fists at his side. "Are you seeing someone in Jacksonville?"

Schooling my features into the best look of boredom I could muster, I replied, "No. I'm at work all the time, or I'm with Rylee." I didn't dare say more than that. Saying more would make me seem defensive.

Scott scrutinized me for a few moments before finally appearing appeased by my answer. He moved to get his own mug out of the cabinet. "I haven't been sleeping with anyone, Sadie. I know the papers make it look otherwise. But I promise you I haven't touched any one of those women."

Snorting, I set my cup down and started to leave the kitchen. "Yeah, okay. I gotta get ready for my meeting with the board for the gala."

"I'm serious, Sadie."

His tone made me pause, and my hackles rose as I turned back to look at him. "Do you think I'm stupid, Scott?"

He walked toward me, both our cups forgotten on the counter. "I was supposed to be out of town for business this weekend. I chartered the jet to bring me back as soon as I saw you were photographed at dinner last night. I wanted to see you. I know I've fucked up in the past, but I swear to you, that's all behind us. I'm here to help you with the charity gala. And I'll explain everything, I promise. We'll go to lunch after the meeting and take a walk in the park afterward. Just like old times."

Scott took my hand between his and raised it to his lips. I stared dumbly as he kissed my knuckles and flashed me that million-dollar smile that had convinced me to marry him after four months of dating. "I love you, baby. You know that. And I know I've been busy with work. I went in on a deal with Mick, and it's taken up a lot of my time-"

"Mick? You went in on a business deal with Mick? I *hate* Mick, Scott. He's a slimy, horrible excuse for a man. You're not doing yourself any favors right now." I ripped my hand from his and stormed down the hall to my bedroom.

Senator Mick Charles and Scott had been buddies long before I had come into the picture. At first, I hadn't wanted to tell Scott that I thought his best friend was an absolute ass. But as time passed, I made it very clear I wanted nothing to do with him.

I also made it very clear that Scott had shared Mick's deepest, darkest secret with me and that I had no problems leaking it to the press if Mick didn't button up his pants and try to be a better husband to his wife, Kate.

Scott followed me as I entered my walk-in closet. He stood in the entrance while I angrily flipped through hanger after hanger in search of a dress for the meeting. "Sadie, this is why I want to explain everything to you, but it's a little hard to do that when you're constantly running down to Jacksonville. If you hadn't shown up this weekend, I'd planned on surprising you down there. You need to stop running away, and we need to fix this."

I faltered at his admission, and again knew he'd picked up on it. After you'd been married for nearly twenty years, you learned each other's tells.

"There's a reason you don't want me down there." A statement, not a question.

"No, there's not. I just happen to like the sun and the ocean. You want me back here more? Fine! I'll start coming back more often," I retorted, exasperated. I ripped a navy vintage Chanel dress off its hanger and moved to find a long jacket to pair with it.

"What I want is for you to act like my *wife!*" Scott yelled, and I felt his ire in my bones.

"Then *you* need to start acting like a fucking husband! Stop fucking everything in a skirt that walks by and flashes you a smile! If that's what you want, then do us both a favor and grant me a fucking divorce! Because I will *not* come back here and be made a fool of!" I threw my clothes on the cream ottoman next to me and sat, pressing my fingers into my temples.

This was why I left New York in the first place.

We couldn't have a normal conversation. My throat already ached with familiarity at the shrillness of my raised voice. My chest heaved, and tears pricked my eyes. I didn't let them fall, but it took effort. I hadn't cried since our last blow-up fight. The one that had caused me to leave New York in search of something more peaceful.

This wasn't home anymore.

Home was cedar and sweet mint and phantom caresses. It was cinnamon and sugar and Rylee's horrible singing. It was the loud din of the bar every night. It was game nights and salty ocean breezes.

And yet... In some small way, deep down, my heart ached to be reunited with the man before me.

Because that's what marriage was.

It was sticking it out through the good and the bad. It was allowing someone to show you their worst selves and still love them for it. Forgiving them for their faults. For better or for worse.

But the bigger part of me kept asking how much worse did it have to get?

How much more did I have to suffer through? I chose this life, yes, but did that mean I had to sit by while Scott decided *when* he wanted to be a good husband?

Why did I have to be the doting wife who looked the other way?

Scott moved toward me slowly, also breathing heavily. I'd never mentioned the 'D' word to him, and from the look on his face, he hadn't expected it.

He sank to his knees when he reached me and gathered my hands in his. "I love you, Sadie. I don't want to divorce you. Can we please just go to the meeting and then to lunch? I just want to talk to you. I have to go back to the West Coast in the morning. Give me the day to explain. *Please*," his tone was earnest as he begged me to spend the day with him.

Scott never begged anyone for anything, yet here he was, on his knees for me, even when it would have been easier for him just to divorce me and let me disappear. But for whatever reason, he was fighting for us–for me.

And I felt myself nod in agreement before I changed my mind.

THE MEETING with the gala board went smoothly. Scott stayed silent throughout it, but supported my suggestions when it mattered. It was amazing what people would fight you on when all you were doing was trying to throw a party to raise money for charity. Two of the women tried to argue over whether or not we should allow seafood to be an ingredient for the hors d'oeuvres.

Scott and I had smirked at each other while they went at it before I straightened and wiped the smile from my face, remembering that he and I weren't in a good place. He didn't seem phased by it, and we'd even had an amicable conversation in the town car as it took us to one of my favorite restaurants for lunch.

"So, what's this deal you went in on with Mick?" I asked between bites of a Caprese salad.

He stiffened for a moment, before replying, "I was hoping to get a few dirty martinis in you before we had that conversation."

Rolling my eyes, I reached for my lemon water while looking around for our waiter so I could order one. "Spit it out, Scott."

"Mick has had a club for years. He started it with

a business partner who isn't cutting it anymore. So, he asked if I'd like to step in and invest. That's all it is, Sadie." He wouldn't meet my eye as he took a bite of his grilled chicken.

I bristled as the waiter appeared, and after ordering my drink, I placed my fork down and leaned back in my chair. "That's what you needed to explain so desperately? That's the reason you've been seen around town with a million other women, Scott? Come on. You used to be able to do much better than that, honey."

A small smile tilted his lips up as he leaned back as well. "The women were auditioning—lower level, emotional only. I haven't touched any one of them, and none of them have been at the penthouse or the apartment."

"Lower level, emotional only, auditions? What does that even mean? What the fuck kind of club is Mick running?" My brows furrowed as I scrunched my nose and fired off questions.

"It's a gentleman's club. Mick thought I'd be a good candidate to see if these women can do what they are being hired to do. Which is just to sit back and listen to the clients."

"In what? Their underwear? So, if that's the lower level, what happens at a higher level? And why the fuck would *you* be a good candidate for auditioning women? Mick's a senator, for fuck's sake. What is he thinking? Does Kate know?"

He raised an eyebrow and gave me a look that

made me snort into the martini that had been placed in front of me. "So, you invested in a sex club?" I asked quietly after taking a sip.

"That isn't what I would call it. And Mick's name isn't on it, not his real name anyway. So, no, Kate doesn't know. That little secret of his? The club is his way of atoning for that. It's all just business. He's had it for twelve years. You know how he is, he may indulge, but I don't. With all the trouble we've been having, he thought it'd be good for me. All I've done is take the women out for a meal and tested their communication skills."

I was about to reply when a rich, friendly tenor cut in. "You're testing someone's communication skills? I'm sorry to tell you this, Uncle, but your communication skills suck."

Turning, I saw Jackson, our nephew on Scott's side, accompanied by his secretary, Stacey. Jackson leaned in to kiss me on the cheek as he said, "Good to see you back in town, Aunt Sadie."

"Good to see you too, Jackson. And you, too, Stacey. Are you keeping the boys in line?" I asked, but already knew the answer to that question. Stacey had been the longest secretary to work for Jackson. Mainly because he couldn't stop sleeping with his and everyone else's, but Stacey didn't like men, and she certainly made it clear to Jackson that she wouldn't abide by him *acting like a male whore on her watch.'*

Her words, not mine.

I respected the hell out of her for it. She'd always told Jackson that when he got older or met someone that mattered to him, he'd regret his sluttish ways. But at thirty-one, Jackson didn't seem to regret anything he did in life.

"You know it, Mrs. Tailor." She narrowed her eyes slightly at Scott before heading to a table.

"Aren't you supposed to be in California?" Jackson asked Scott.

"I'm going back in the morning. I just came back for the day to spend it with your aunt. So, if you don't mind, scram." Scott sounded annoyed and I wondered if he and Jackson were fighting again.

Jackson was a bit of a loose cannon. His father, Scott's brother, took his life when Jackson was just a baby, and his mother had never been in the picture past giving birth. Scott's mom had taken him in and raised him, and as soon as he'd graduated college, Scott had taken him under his wing. But all the money had gone to Jackson's head, and he liked to show off with lavish parties and a different model on his arm every weekend.

Scott said it was bad for their business's image.

I think Scott was just jealous that it wasn't *his* life anymore.

Even though, clearly, it was. And Scott chastising someone for giving their business a bad name? Pot, meet kettle.

Jackson laughed and waggled his eyebrows at us. "Okay, okay! Have fun, kids."

We were quiet as we watched him walk away and join Stacey at their table.

Finally, after what seemed like forever, I broke the silence. "You know, he's not wrong. You do suck at communication. And I don't know how I feel about you *auditioning* women and talking about our private life with random strangers."

I thought about how I'd done the same with Tyler, which made me realize I still hadn't responded to his message. I didn't know how to reply, especially with Scott over my shoulder all day.

Like I needed him to see a picture of another man's dick on my phone. Talk about being a hypocrite.

That realization caused me to soften, at the same moment, Scott reached across the table and took my hand in his. "If you don't want me to do it anymore, I won't. But it's been lonely here without you, Sadie. Not that it's any excuse. I guess I was acting out for attention. You seem pretty content with leaving your life here behind for the beach."

"My job is there."

"You don't need to work, and you know it."

I shrugged and drained my glass, picking up the toothpick that held three green olives—just how I liked it. "I like what I do. It gives me a purpose other than being a trophy wife."

Scott appraised me carefully like he was searching for the answer to a complicated question. He knew my tells, and I'd already given two instances in which Tyler had occupied my mind when he asked me questions, and I fed him lies in return.

The shrill ring of his phone interrupted the lull in our conversation, and I'd never been more grateful for one of his work calls. After he answered it, he covered the speaker briefly and leaned closer. "Would you mind if I ran to the office real quick? I'll meet you at home in an hour. I promise."

I nodded and gave him a tight smile. "Of course, duty calls."

Just like it always did whenever we were supposed to have time together.

He flashed me an appreciative smile as he stood from the table, kissing my forehead before he resumed his conversation as he made his way out of the building.

I didn't leave the restaurant until two more martinis gave me enough courage to *love* the photo Tyler sent me.

SCOTT HADN'T RETURNED HOME after an hour. I currently sat at my giant vanity, idly playing with the sash of my black silk robe while wondering if he'd be home in time for our dinner reservations.

While I waited, I'd curled my hair in soft waves, the length skimming just below my collarbone now that it was growing out. I'd put on more makeup than

I had in the last year combined and dressed in my best black lace-topped stockings and lingerie to go under my strapless chiffon-draped mini from Oscar de la Renta.

I grabbed my phone, ready to send a message to Tyler to see what he was doing, when Scott's image appeared in the vanity mirror. The look on his face was remorseful, like he was prepared for my anger at the fact that he hadn't come home or so much as called to let me know not to wait for him. In his hands was a long rectangular box—jewelry, no doubt, his usual white flag.

"I'm sorry I didn't make it home when I said I would," he spoke softly, slowly walking further into the room until he stood right behind me, our gazes locked in the mirror.

"It's fine. Nothing I'm not used to. You are—if anything—predictable that way." I tried to keep the bite from my tone but failed miserably.

He broke our gaze and looked down at the carpet. "I deserved that, and you deserve better. I'm sorry. Not that this will make up for it, but I got you a gift."

My heart jumped. Even though it wasn't a fact I was proud of, my number one love language was gifts. The second was physical touch, and Scott knew how to use both to his advantage and make me a puddle in his greedy hands. Turning in my seat, I tried not to appear *too* eager. But Scott noticed and chuckled as he raised the box.

My breath caught as he opened the lid, revealing carat-sized opulent emerald-cut diamonds stretched out in three pliant rows. They were caged in by two rows of princess-cut champagne diamonds, all set in platinum. At first glance, I thought it was a wide wrist cuff, but as I gently touched it, Scott picked up one end and motioned for me to turn around. I did as he silently asked, the breath in my throat tight as he gently moved my hair to the side to secure the statement piece.

A choker.

The symbolism wasn't lost on me as I admired the necklace that now took up almost half of my neck. I swallowed, the diamonds sparkling with the movement. "Scott, this is...what is this for?"

He smiled and gently kissed the side of my neck before pressing his cheek to mine as we locked eyes in the mirror. "I don't need a reason to buy my wife Harry Winston. But I'm sure you're guessing it's an apology, and you'd be right. I'm sorry for humiliating you. I'm going to spend a very long time making it up to you."

Scott reached around me, much like Tyler had in the office at Sugar and Scotch, his hands reaching for the hem of my robe as he nuzzled my neck. Once he dragged my robe up enough to reveal the tops of my stockings, he groaned, and the faint scent of cigar smoke filled my nose.

It was all wrong. Nothing like the cedar and

sweet mint I'd come to crave. But if I closed my eyes...

"Open your eyes and look at me, Sadie," Scott commanded huskily. He gripped my chin and pulled my head to the side to seal our lips together, my body igniting as his fingers found their way between my legs. I made a mewling noise against his lips as his tongue sought out mine, his fingers running up my center over the lace of my thong.

He released me suddenly as I moved to stand, my hands finding the sash of my robe before slowly untying it. Scott swallowed, his Adam's apple bobbing as he watched while I parted the silk to reveal the lingerie underneath. I caught a glimpse of myself in one of the full-length mirrors across the room, nearly naked save for the tiny scraps of black silk and lace and the diamond choker.

"Fuck, I missed you," Scott breathed out, reaching up to loosen his tie.

Years ago, I had told myself that I wouldn't ever let him make a fool out of me.

I lied.

I'd said I wasn't stupid enough to return to New York and have sex with him.

Another lie.

And as I helped him out of his jacket and began frantically unbuttoning his dress shirt, I told myself that he was being truthful and that he hadn't really been sleeping with any other women.

I was wound so fucking tight with tension

because of Tyler. I needed a release, and Scott knew exactly how to give my body what it craved. So, I fucked him on the ottoman in our walk-in closet, before doing it repeatedly in our bed throughout the night until we were satiated.

And even when the rest of my clothing disappeared...the diamonds had remained.

Lust was a shallow bitch, and apparently, so was I.

CHAPTER SIX

I woke to the sounds of Scott rushing around the room. The weight of the diamonds around my neck felt like a crushing grip matched by the feeling in my chest. I rolled onto my back, sitting up to secure the sheet around my chest before removing the necklace.

"Good morning," Scott said before I felt the press of his lips against the crown of my head. "I have to go. I was supposed to leave an hour ago."

"Whatever will the businessmen of Los Angeles do without you?" I lilted as I watched him button up a crisp, white dress shirt.

"I told them I couldn't leave until my wife had been fully satisfied." He smirked at me as he moved on to his tie.

I stood from the bed in all my naked glory and reached up to help him. "Consider your wife satisfied," I remarked softly.

Satisfied and confused, if I were being honest.

Every fiber in my being longed to talk to Tyler. I was having trouble differentiating whether that was because he'd become my emotional crutch or because I'd pictured his dick while riding Scott's the night before.

Scott's hands drifted to my hips, and he stepped into me as I folded his collar over the tie before winding my arms around his neck. "Will you come back next weekend?" he asked.

Sighing, I shook my head slightly. "Chance and Rylee have family coming into town for the weekend. I need to take care of the bakery."

One of his hands slowly skimmed my side as it made its way up my body, leaving goosebumps in its wake. He trailed his fingers lightly over the side of my breast before coming back down to flick over my nipple. "Maybe I'll come down there then."

I could feel the strain of his erection through his dress pants and quickly thought of an appeasing answer that wouldn't have him questioning why I didn't want him to visit Jacksonville. "You hate the beach. And I'm going to be at the bar all weekend. You hate sitting at a bar. Don't punish yourself, Scott. I'll come back the following weekend, I promise."

Leaning closer, I threaded my hands in his hair and kissed him thoroughly before pulling back. "You'd better get going. You're already late."

AS SOON AS SCOTT LEFT, I made my way to the kitchen for a cup of coffee. Claudia hummed away as I then walked back to my room, and into the closet, with my mug and the necklace to put back in its box. "Good morning, Claudia."

"Good morning, Mrs. Sadie. How was your evening?" she asked as she bent to grab Scott's discarded clothes from the floor. A card fell out of his jacket as she stood. It was black with a silver design and looked heavy.

Setting my coffee and the necklace down on my vanity, I bent to grab it. "What's this?"

I didn't expect her to know, I was more talking to myself, but she turned, and the look on her face when she saw what I held was enough to let me know that she knew exactly what it was.

The card looked like a hotel room key. It was matte black with a shiny platinum feather embossed on one side and a plain black magnetic strip on the other. I looked from her back to the card and then again at the plump lady I'd come to consider family. She'd worked for us for over fifteen years, after all.

"Claudia, do you know what this is?" A weight settled in my chest. The nagging feeling that Scott had been lying all along crept down the base of my spine.

She took a deep breath and started to shake her head. "I told Mr. Scott to tell you the whole truth, but I'm guessing he did not if you are asking me what that is."

My brows furrowed. "Does this have something to do with Mick's club?"

She jerked her head at the card before she turned to leave. "Use a blacklight on the back of the card and find your answers there, Mrs. Sadie. I don't want to get caught in the middle of yours and Mr. Scott's games."

As if she'd backhanded me, I blanched and took a step back. "*My* games?"

I followed her as she walked down the hall. She made a brief stop to hang Scott's clothes so she could take them to be dry cleaned, before resuming her trek to Scott's in-home office. "Your phone has been going off all morning. You're lucky Mr. Scott didn't bother looking at it. You have your secrets, too, Mrs. Sadie. You are not innocent," she scolded as she dug around in the desk drawer.

Words escaped me, so I turned to go grab my phone from its place by my purse in the foyer to see multiple texts lit up on my lock screen. Most were from my group chat with Rylee, Chance, and Tyler. There were a few from various gossip column writers asking for details on the status of Scott's and my marriage. But right at the top was what Claudia must have been talking about.

In big capital letters, there was a message from Tyler. Followed by two more in a regular-sized font.

Why the fuck hadn't I remembered to turn off the previews?

Groaning, I turned to see Claudia standing right behind me with a raised brow. She held out a small black object that looked like a pen and clicked the end of it, a small blue light illuminating the tip.

I took it from her, and she walked away without another word.

"We don't pay you enough," I called down the hall after her.

While she made sounds of agreement, I sighed, tossing my phone in my purse, then flipped the card over and shined the light on it. An address glowed brightly against the metal, along with a name.

Carmela.

My hackles raised and I grabbed my phone again to look up the address, puzzled when a restaurant we'd invested in years ago popped up on my screen.

Decadence, an exquisite French bistro a few blocks from Central Park.

Glancing at the clock, I saw that it was barely ten. My flight didn't leave until one that afternoon, and the restaurant opened at eleven. If I hurried, I could find out who this Carmela was and hopefully get some answers about what, exactly, Scott had been up to.

"GOOD AFTERNOON. Will it just be you today?" a pretty hostess, too young to have had her hopes and dreams dashed by the city yet, asked me as I walked in.

Taking off my sunglasses, I looked around at the small space. It was just as I remembered—all modern and industrial exposed brick, distressed wood with bronzed metal furnishings, and large geometric pendant lighting. There were no customers yet, and I could only see one young waitress with long, rich-coppery hair doing side work in the back near the open-concept kitchen.

"I'm looking for Carmela," I told her.

She didn't skip a beat as she smiled and shook her head. "I'm sorry, we don't have anyone here by that name."

I huffed a laugh and flashed the card I'd kept with me. The hostess visibly stiffened and her eyes widened.

"You can tell her Sadie Tailor wants to speak with her," I asserted, before heading to a table in the far corner next to a large window.

The redheaded waitress made eye contact with me as the hostess went and whispered in her ear. As she walked over, I slid the card on the table, feather side up. The redhead looked at it nervously as she approached, before she schooled her features and turned her cornflower-blue eyes to mine. There was a curious gleam in them as she appraised me without trying to seem obvious about it.

"Hi there, what can I get you?" she asked as she poured me a glass of ice water.

"I'll take a flat white while I wait. Thank you, Scarlett," I answered, reading the name on her name tag.

She blinked before she turned and left without another word. Once she'd brought me my espresso, it only took another ten minutes of people-watching before someone cleared their throat.

I turned to see a woman with tan skin and glossy black hair that reached the middle of her back. She wore black dress pants with black pumps and a deep red silk blouse. Her eyes were dark as they took me in, and darkened further when they saw the card on the table. She sat across from me, and I noticed she looked as tense as I felt.

"You must be Carmela."

"Mrs. Tailor. Your husband didn't inform me he'd be bringing you into all this." She got straight to the point.

"My husband isn't aware I'm here. This fell out of his suit jacket, and our housekeeper knew how to find the message on the back. So, tell me, Carmela, what is *all this?*"

She looked dubious for a moment before reply-ing, "Probably not what you think it is. We work together, that's it. We've barely spoken, to be honest. Usually, I just deal with Mick."

"So this *does* have to do with their club?" Typi-cally, I'd have a hard time believing Scott barely spoke to her if they worked together, but the look on her face told me she was just as sick of those two men as I was.

"*My* club. Mick is barely involved, and your husband, while more hands-on, is just filling in for a while at Mick's insistence."

I stiffened at her words, and she winced, no doubt realizing why. "Hands-on, hmm?" I had the sudden urge to hide behind my sunglasses in humiliation.

"Not like that. I'm sorry, that came out wrong." The waitress interrupted her as she set a cup down in front of Carmela. I didn't recall her ordering anything, but there was now a steaming chai latte before her, complete with a cinnamon-shaped leaf on the top.

"Thank you, Ginny," she said.

Both she and the red-haired girl tensed for a moment. I would have missed it if I hadn't been watching their interaction so closely. Their actions, paired with the fact that the name Carmela used didn't match the waitress's name tag, made me think she worked at their little club.

I tensed my jaw and wondered if this waitress

had ever slept with my husband, remembering when Scott had been photographed with a redhead a few months back.

Carmela quickly recovered and gave a slight shrug as *Ginny* walked away. "Her name is on her name tag."

"Right. You must think I'm stupid. As a woman yourself, you'd think you wouldn't be in the business of humiliating other women," I snapped.

"On the contrary, I try to empower women. What men do at the club isn't my fault or my girls'. Unfaithful men will be unfaithful, whether at my club or somewhere else."

"And Scott? Has he *auditioned* Gingersnap over there? Or any of the other girls at your club?" I bit the inside of my cheek after asking the question. My heart raced in anticipation of her answer, to know whether my husband was being truthful or if I had fallen for more of his lies.

Her eyes softened for a moment before she shook her head. "To my knowledge, Scott hasn't been with any of the girls at the club. He's taken our lowest tier of women out to see if they can converse, that's all."

I let out the breath I'd been holding. Adrenaline pumped through my veins at a rapid pace, which caused my body to tingle with a heavy feeling of relief.

Scott hadn't lied to me about anything.

He'd been telling the truth.

Carmela had corroborated Scott's story under no

obligation or loyalty to him. And I decided then that I needed to give him the chance he'd been so desperately asking for yesterday.

A strange feeling, equal parts relieved and anxious, flowed through me. I would have to go back to Jacksonville and talk seriously with Tyler about the boundaries of our friendship, and with Rylee about the future of my involvement with Sugar and Scotch–if I were to stick to my word and return to New York more often.

"I know we don't know each other, but I feel obligated to tell you." Carmela's voice snapped me out of my reverie, and my eyes found hers across the table. She looked like she was about to tell me someone had died, and the anxiousness chased away the relief in my gut.

"Scott may not seek companionship from any of *our* girls, but the circles run small, and people *do* talk. Your husband is not faithful to you, Mrs. Tailor. As a matter of fact, he took a girl with him to California on Friday, and another went with him this morning."

She avoided my eyes as she told me, and for that, I was grateful. I could feel the telltale prickling of tears in my eyes, and the unmistakable, choking burn in the back of my throat as I attempted to keep them at bay. My body felt numb, all the previous emotions turning to lead in my stomach.

And then I realized that we hadn't used protection last night, and felt dirty despite my earlier shower. I would need to see my doctor immediately to get tested to make sure Scott hadn't given me any STIs.

I felt like a fool.

In the words of Daisy Buchanan, a beautiful little fool.

CHAPTER SEVEN

Tyler

I WAS FULLY CONVINCED SCOTT HAD EITHER shown up in New York without her knowing or Sadie had lied to me about him being out of town.

She'd never gone this long without texting me. Her fucking heart emoji on the photo I sent her of my cock was like a slap in the face. A slap that should have woken my stupid ass up, but my sister always told me I was pretty, so I didn't have to be smart.

Something was wrong.

I thought about sending her another message, but I'd already sent her three this morning and two this afternoon, wondering where she was. She was supposed to be on a one o'clock flight back, but it was nearing four, and no one had heard from her, including Rylee.

The sound of the door to my house opening pulled my attention over my shoulder to see Chance coming in with a giddy grin. "I got it," he sang out.

I smiled and was about to respond, when the sound of someone FaceTiming me went off. Whipping around, I saw Sadie's number on my screen and answered it quickly.

"I was beginning to think you'd died." My nerves were frayed, and my stomach clenched in a giant knot as her image came on the screen.

"Is that Sadie?" Chance asked as he appeared over my shoulder and waved to the phone. "I got the ring!" He pulled the stool beside mine closer and placed the ring box on the island between us.

"I know. I'm sorry. Some things came up. I'm at the airport now. I'm catching a five o'clock flight. What did Chance say? I didn't hear him over the intercom," she answered calmly. Like she hadn't been ignoring everyone for days. I propped my phone against the paper towel holder and took in her appearance.

She looked frazzled. Her hair was mussed, like she'd been running her hands through it all day—or how I imagined it would look after she'd been thoroughly fucked. Her eyes were bloodshot, and she was chewing on her lip—a nervous trait of hers.

Something was definitely wrong.

Chance bumped his shoulder into mine to fit into the small frame on the screen. His dopey grin was a glaring contrast to the annoyed downturn of my lips. I leaned over and flipped the hood of my zip-up over my head, as he opened the red leather ring box and held it up for us to see.

The ring was very Rylee. Set in platinum, the stone was an elongated cushion-cut pink diamond, with a baguette diamond on each side, and smaller diamonds down the band.

How did I know the technical terms, you might ask?

Chance made me go with him every time he went and talked to the jeweler. I knew more about diamonds now than I'd ever imagined I would.

Instead of gushing over the ring, Sadie smiled sadly at the camera and gave a short nod. "It's really pretty, Chance."

I'd told him he should have included her in the design of it, but Chance wanted to do it all on his own. At first, I thought maybe she was sad because he hadn't asked her, but the way she acted only affirmed that something else was bothering her.

"Are you okay, Sadie?"

"What's wrong? You don't think she'll like it?" Chance asked at the same time.

She ignored my question, even though her eyes snapped to mine at the use of her name. I rarely called her Sadie. Always Wifey. So when I did use her name, she knew I meant business.

Her eyes found Chance's again as she said, "I think she'll love it. You did good. It's just.... Not to channel Miranda or anything, and trust me, you're as far away from being John Preston as you could be— you're actually more like Aidan, who *should* have ended up with Carrie, but I'm getting off track here.

I just think you guys can still have your happily ever after without a marriage certificate."

While she was speaking, she looked everywhere *but* the camera, as she waved her hands around like they would help her get her point across. Chance glanced at me with a look that said, *'what is she talking about?'*

I checked to see her still waving her hands around and not looking at us as she spoke, so I looked back at him and shrugged, shaking my head.

This was one of those moments where our age difference was thrown in our faces. Neither of us had any clue who these people she was talking about were.

"It's just an expensive piece of paper if you decide you don't mesh well in ten years. That's all I'm saying," she finished.

We were silent for a moment before Chance spoke up, his tone laced with agitation. "So, you're telling me I shouldn't ask her to marry me?"

Sadie shook her head and sighed. "Just giving you another point of view, Chance. That's all."

"Thanks," he deadpanned. "I thought you'd be happier for us, Sadie."

I shifted in my seat and grabbed my phone before Sadie could respond. "Hey, let me talk to her. I'll see you later," I told him, sliding off my stool and heading to my bedroom. As I walked down the hall, I lifted my phone to see Sadie looking like she wanted to cry.

"Hey," I said softly. "What's going on?"

Her eyes lined with tears and she blinked furiously to keep them from falling. She started to fan herself and plastered a fake smile on her face. "It's just been a day. I'm ready to be home."

"Do you want to talk about it? It seems like you need to." I got on my bed and threw my other arm on my pillow behind my head. "You know I'm here to listen."

"Tyler, can we just *not* right now? Please? I don't need to lose my shit in the middle of the Chelsea Lounge."

I stiffened momentarily, before allowing a silly grin to pull my lips up. "Aww, why you gotta be so mean to me, Wifey? I'm just trying to make you feel better!"

A mask. A charade I'd gotten too good at performing. I'd mastered how to be whatever she needed in the moments we were together. Even if it was a dangerous game I played with my own feelings.

Sadie had awakened a part of me I thought was long gone. String after string of bad relationships and women who couldn't handle me—all of them leaving after making me feel like shit about myself.

I was too much.

I wasn't enough.

And even though I was young, it had still put me in a headspace where I believed I wasn't cut out for relationships or capable of making a woman happy.

But the closer Chance and Rylee had grown, so had Sadie and I. She made me feel alive. She laughed at my jokes and encouraged my stupid antics, mainly when they were targeting Chance and Rylee. She never got annoyed with me and accepted me for me.

And the way she responded to my intensity made my fucking blood sing.

"I know you are. I'm sorry, Pup. I just need a drink and a nice long chat with Rylee. I'll be in a better mood by the time I land. I'll see you later?" she asked before she looked away and ordered a dirty martini.

"Sure thing. See you in a little bit."

"Bye, Pup."

We ended the call. I ran my hand over my face and took a deep breath. If she wanted to talk to Rylee, she needed to talk about Scott, and then she'd want to spend the night drinking with me, because that had become her routine. She vented to Rylee about how shitty her husband was and then sought emotional comfort with me, because I made her feel safe—even if she didn't want to admit that last part out loud.

That was the thing, though. She didn't need to admit it out loud because I already knew. It was only a matter of time before her resolve crumbled and she gave in to her feelings for me. Because for as much as she had pulled me out of a dark place, I think I'd done the same for her.

Only, when she finally gave in, I knew it would ruin us, since there was no way in hell her husband would ever let her go. However, that wouldn't stop me from holding on to the fragments of happiness we provided each other.

Ours was a love story that had yet to be written but was already outlined to have a tragic ending.

CHAPTER EIGHT

AFTER GOING HOME TO CHANGE ONCE I GOT OFF the plane, I went to Sugar and Scotch in search of my best friend. With me going to New York more often now, we'd hired another bartender, so I didn't have to be there as much, but I'd still dressed in a work outfit in case I decided to blow off some steam by making drinks.

I knew Tyler would eventually make his way in tonight, and I was feeling petty after everything I'd learned about Scott today, so I dressed to impress. Tight, black leather pants with a matching corseted top, and black suede ankle boots. One of Tyler's favorite outfits of mine. I'd curled my hair to hang down in messy, effortless-looking curls and applied a red lipstick that usually only saw the light of day in New York.

It was a confidence boost since I'd spent the afternoon feeling like shit about myself. I'd been continuously comparing my *older* looks to that of Carmela and Ginny since I left Decadence.

Thoughts of why Scott would stay married to me, when he was being kept company by women who looked like *them,* had plagued my brain the entire flight back to Jacksonville. And while Tyler's compliments and attention had always made me feel better about myself, I *wanted* to feed into it tonight.

Walking into the back of Sugar and Scotch, I immediately sought Rylee, who was focused intently on decorating a wedding cake that she and Chance were delivering tomorrow. Her hair was piled on top of her head, and her frilly pink apron was covered in lavender frosting and luster dust.

As soon as she saw me, she smiled and set down the sugar hydrangea she was about to place. "Welcome home! How was New York?!" she asked as she hugged me.

My gaze shifted over to the night cooks who were minding their own business, like they usually did whenever Rylee was working late, and then I nodded to the cake and asked her, "Do you have a minute to talk in the office?"

A worried look crossed her face. "Is everything okay? Oh my God, don't tell me you're moving back there."

Grabbing her hand, I pulled her down the hall, closing the door once inside. "No, I'm not moving back. But...a lot happened while I was there this weekend. Scott showed up."

"Oh no. Sadie, I know that look. Please tell me you didn't." She dropped into her chair as I sat in mine and ran a hand through my hair, mussing up my curls and letting out a big sigh.

"I did. And I'm not proud of it. But that isn't even the worst thing." I spent the next ten minutes explaining what had happened between Scott and me, about finding the card for the club, and confronting Carmela.

"And honestly, this whole time, I have felt fucking terrible for wanting Tyler as much as I do, but now? Fuck it. I'm done. Scott can have his whores. I'm going to stop beating myself up over wanting to explore this thing between Tyler and me." I finished my story with a flourish as I leaned back in my chair and took in Rylee's unreadable expression.

"Your life in New York is so much different than here. It's crazy. I keep having to remind myself this is your life and that you're not reading a chapter from a fictional book. He bought you a diamond *choker,* for fuck's sake. Did he plan on taking you to this new club of his and attaching a leash?" She was clearly disgusted, but I knew it was with Scott's intentions and not with me.

"You know, I never even thought of that. Honestly, it's a beautiful piece. New York Sadie was more than happy to wear it while being fucked. But even though I believed his bullshit at the time, I still thought of Tyler while I did it," I admitted.

"Girl, it is about damn time. That boy probably has the bluest balls by now. Well, actually, I guess not if he's jerking off in the shower and sending you pictures. Oh my God, I didn't need to picture that," she said as she squeezed her eyes shut and shook her head vigorously. "He's like a little brother. I cannot, and will not, picture that! Bleh!" She stuck out her tongue and grimaced.

We both laughed before she shot me a serious look. "Are you going to tell Scott you know he's lying to you?"

I thought about it for a moment. I'd been asking myself the same question. Was I ready to ask Scott for a divorce and start the nasty battle that would be inevitable? I honestly didn't know the answer.

"Not yet. If I decide to say anything, it won't be until after the gala." I contemplated my next question, unsure if I was ready to hear Rylee's honest answer.

After a few moments, I relented and asked in a rush of words, "Do you think I'm a bad person for dragging Tyler into this?"

She furrowed her brow before shaking her head as she stood and came to stand in front of me. Grabbing my shoulders, she looked me dead in the eyes and replied, "Absolutely not, Sadie. Tyler has known this entire time that you're married. He's a big boy. He knew what he was getting himself into. Do not make yourself feel bad about this. You guys are grown adults, and you've agonized over your feelings while your husband has been actively fucking other women and lying to you about it. Stop feeling bad. Is cheating good? No. Is it the end of the world? Also, no. Once the gala is over, you can talk to Scott and figure out where to go after that. Until then, enjoy Tyler! I'm sure you already know, but trust me, that boy is more than ready to take you for a ride on his joystick."

I snorted as she straightened up and headed for the door. "It's more like a pogo stick."

Her hands flew over her ears, and she started yelling, "La la la la la, I can't hear you!"

THE NEW BARTENDER was a dark-skinned beauty named Riya. Her hair was cut close to her head in a shocking shade of blonde that was almost white. She was only an inch or two shorter than me, around Tyler's height, and looked every bit like a perfect runway model.

Before I could sit on the stool closest to the doors that led to the back, she placed a dirty martini on the bar top, her magenta-painted lips upturned in a full smile. "Nice to finally meet you, Sadie."

I moaned after taking a sip of my drink and slapped the top of the bar. "Yes! You stirred it! Good girl. Why is it that no one ever gets that?" I took another sip as she laughed. Remembering my manners, I followed up with, "It's good to meet you too. I'm sorry I wasn't here to train you, but something tells me you don't need any training."

"I was in Vegas before this. Worked at a lot of martini bars," she explained while pouring someone a beer. The place was fairly busy, but she didn't look like she was even mildly struggling with the number of people patiently waiting for her to get their orders.

"What brought you here?" I asked, before popping one of the olives in my mouth.

"Just ready for a new adventure, I guess. Something a little quieter," she answered, before moving to the end of the bar to make a group of people's shots.

Finishing my drink, I observed how effortlessly she took care of customers, knowing that Rylee had one hundred percent made the right choice in hiring her. I checked my phone to see if Tyler had messaged me at all, but the only message I'd received in the last two hours had been from Scott, telling me he missed me already and was looking forward to the next weekend we'd see each other.

Huffing, I ignored it. I wasn't going to New York in two weeks. I'd make up another excuse like I always did.

I checked my email to see if the lab results had come back from my blood panel and swabs I'd had taken at the doctor earlier—they hadn't. I'd pushed my flight back so my regular doctor could squeeze me in. I would have been desperate enough to go into a walk-in clinic, but I loved my doctor, and she, along with the rest of her office, had already signed NDAs.

Riya's voice cut through my thoughts as I exited my mail app. "So... Rylee's boyfriend Chance, you're close with his friend Tyler, right?"

Immediately, I tensed and raised my eyes to meet hers. "Yeah, we are." There was an edge of warning to my voice as I spoke.

"Could you introduce me to that pretty blonde that's been staying with him all weekend?" She looked down at the far end of the bar.

My hackles raised as I followed her line of sight to see Tyler as he walked through the entrance at the other end, where the new pool tables we'd just bought were. Next to him was a honey-blonde, blue-eyed bombshell of a girl. She looked his age, and the way she smiled up at him with her pearly whites was enough to make me see red.

"I'm sorry, what? She's been staying with him all weekend?" I asked in a tight voice.

But I didn't wait for her to answer as Tyler's head turned our way for a second and back to the petite woman.

He'd completely ignored me.

Irrational rage coursed through my veins. Later, I would remind myself that Tyler was single and could do whatever he wanted, that it was none of my business.

But right now?

I was fucking livid.

I caught the eye of the woman first as I marched over to them. She looked me up and down as she realized I was headed in their direction and raised an eyebrow as if to say, '*what's your problem?*'

"Tyler. Care to introduce me to whoever you've been sleeping with all weekend?" I bit out in an accusing tone.

He jumped and turned around to see me standing there with my hands on my hips. "Sadie. I didn't see you when we came in–"

"Yeah, I'm sure. You looked right at me. So? Who the fuck is this?" I cut him off as my eyes found hers.

"Who the fuck are *you*?" she scoffed. "Tyler, *please* do not tell me this is her."

"Oh, so you know about me, that's great. Guess the fucking joke is on me, then. Huh, Pup? Didn't think you were the type, but good to know that I was wrong."

Tyler shook his head. "Sadie, stop. *Now*." His voice was low, gravelly, and authoritative.

He'd never used that tone with me, and I was ashamed to admit it did things to my insides, even in our current situation.

"You have it all wrong," he continued. "This is Ashlee. My *sister*."

"And you are fucking crazy. You know, when he told me he was obsessed with a married woman, I told him he was stupid, but Jesus Christ, Tyler. She's fucking insane," she followed up.

My cheeks hurt from the shade of crimson that

now colored my face, and my mouth opened and closed like a fish out of water. I looked over to see Rylee and Riya as they, along with most of the bar, looked at me wide-eyed.

Turning my gaze back to Tyler, I found him staring at me with something in his eyes akin to disappointment as he clenched and unclenched his jaw repeatedly.

"Your sister? You didn't mention your sister was coming to town this weekend. Rylee didn't mention it either," I remarked. Embarrassment danced along my limbs, and my skin felt hot from the flush getting worse the longer I stood there.

"If you'd bothered to check the group chat, you would have seen that we did. Even sent a photo of all of us at Chance and Rylee's," he pointed out quietly.

My gaze fell to a random spot on the floor. I could barely look at Tyler's sister as I uttered a scarcely audible, "I'm sorry." Then bolted for the back.

As I walked the length of the room, everyone snapped back to what they were doing as Rylee rushed toward me. "I'm so sorry, Sadie. I assumed you knew. We were blowing up the group chat all weekend," she exclaimed.

"No, it's fine. It's my fault." I rounded the bar to head to the back, my eyes finding Riya's as I shrugged. "I think you're better off introducing yourself."

She gave me an empathetic look as I pushed my

way through the doors to the back. I could hear Rylee and Tyler exchanging heated words while I made my way down the hall to grab my purse and keys to go home.

Shame and guilt racked my body as I realized I'd never even seen a picture of Tyler's sister in all the months we'd been hanging out. I knew they were close, but what did that say about me? To have never even asked.

I was selfish and stupid, and first impressions were everything. There would be no coming back from the scene I'd just caused. Seconds after I entered the office to grab my stuff, the door slammed behind me, and I spun around to see Tyler standing there. His chest heaved with every breath, and his midnight eyes locked intensely on mine. After a few moments of us just staring at each other, his tone was low and husky as he finally said, "You were jealous."

Swallowing thickly, I nodded my head ever so slightly and confirmed his statement. He didn't say anything else as he started walking toward me slowly. For every step he took, I took one in the opposite direction, earning me a devilish smirk from him.

My back eventually hit the wall, but Tyler didn't stop his advancement until we were nearly chest-to-chest. He was only an inch and a half shorter than I was—we'd measured once—but I felt so small as he lifted his arms and rested them on the wall, effectively caging me in.

"You looked right at me, and you ignored me. I

just snapped. I'm sorry. I know I have no right." My voice was quiet and sounded pitiful.

"Sadie, I didn't see you. I glanced over momentarily and saw that it *wasn't* you behind the bar. I didn't look to see who was sitting at it. And you have *every* right. You have since I first called you Wifey." He was so close, and my eyes darted down to his lips as he spoke. I wanted to feel them against mine for more than the second we shared what now seemed like a lifetime ago.

"You're ready, aren't you? Something happened in New York to change your mind," he speculated into the space between us.

He leaned closer, and the stubble from his beard skimmed along my cheek until his lips ghosted my ear. "I don't know if I want to know what made you realize it, but it's about damn time. Now, tell me."

One of his hands skimmed slowly, gently down my side, and my breathing hitched. "Tell you what?" I asked with a breathy moan. My hands raised and fisted in his dark gray Henley, right over his heart, and I could feel it beating as fast as mine.

Liquid warmth pooled between my legs as his lips barely touched the skin beneath my ear, and he pulled one of my legs up around his hip, pressing me into the wall. I could feel his cock as it strained against his pants, and I desperately wanted to reach down and run my hand along it.

I bit my lip as he pulled his head back, and he let out a groan before resting his forehead on mine. "Tell me how badly you want me, Sadie. Tell me how badly you want this." He rocked his hips into me, and I threw my head back as his cock rubbed just right against my clit through our pants. My whole body felt like it had been electrified, and I smiled with euphoric satisfaction.

The hand still resting on my hip gripped me harder, and he rocked his hips again, more gently this time. "Look at me, Sadie. I want to see your face when you tell me how badly you want my cock."

I obeyed him, and my breathing stuttered when my hips moved against his, causing both of us to let out low moans. "I want you, Tyler. I want you so fucking bad it hurts."

He paused as his eyes widened slightly in shock, as if he hadn't really expected me to admit it. It didn't take him long to recover, and he rewarded me with a genuine smile as his gaze dropped to my lips, and he surged forward to kiss me.

Before he could, I admitted in a hoarse voice, "But I need to tell you, I slept with Scott in New York."

The passion died in his eyes as quickly as putting out a flame from a candle. It felt like a cold bucket of water had doused us as he dropped my leg and backed away, as if I'd physically hit him.

Pushing off the wall, I moved closer, but he held up a hand to stop me as he ran the other one through his hair. "I fucking knew it. I knew something was up with you this weekend."

"I'm sorry. I'm so sorry, Tyler." I felt so fucking guilty for not telling him as soon as I'd woken up that morning. He'd at least deserved that.

He barked a laugh, and it startled me enough that I jumped. "Don't apologize for fucking your husband, Sadie. But forgive me if I don't want Scott's sloppy seconds."

My breath caught in my throat, and I was too stunned to say anything as Tyler turned, opened the door, and walked out. Tears lined my eyes, and I finally let them fall for the first time today.

Rylee appeared as a blurry, pink blob moments later, and I heard her gentle words of comfort as I crumpled to the ground and cried for the woman I'd become.

"It's going to be okay, Sadie. I promise it will all be okay. Don't cry," Rylee soothed.

"Oh, shit. Okay. We're going to need a lot of alcohol for this. I'm gonna announce last call," Riya's voice rang out a few minutes later after she entered the office and saw me on the floor.

Eventually, my sobs subsided, and I picked myself up with Rylee's help. "I don't want to talk about it," I grumbled, unable to meet her eyes.

"You don't have to, babe. Whenever you're ready, you know I'm here to listen. But Tyler looked really upset when he left. Just tell me you're okay?" she requested.

"As okay as I knew I would be when this all blew up in my face." I breathed through a fresh batch of silent tears. A movement to my right pulled my attention to Riya as she re-entered the office with a bottle of strawberry Cruzan and a pint of vanilla Talenti.

"Every bar should have it for occasions just like this," she explained softly as she set it down between Rylee and me, along with two spoons.

She left without another word, and I looked at Rylee, picking up a spoon and unscrewing the lid from the gelato. "I like her. Can she stay forever?"

CHAPTER NINE

Tyler

To her credit, Ashlee was fairly quiet as I drove her to the airport. However, as we pulled up to JAX, she looked at me and sighed. "Alright, we gotta talk about it, Ty."

I didn't want to talk about it. The second I'd pushed through the doors that connected the back to the bar, all I'd wanted to do was turn around and tell Sadie it was fine. That I wasn't mad, and I didn't mean what I'd said to her.

Truthfully, I wasn't even mad that she'd slept with him. He was her husband, after all. I was angry because he continuously slept around on her and treated her like shit.

I treated her like the goddess she was and hadn't so much as looked at another woman since I met her.

It made me sick that she would let him touch her but wouldn't allow me to show her she deserved, and could have, better.

"She made a mistake. Under different circumstances, I promise you'd like her, Ash," I told her.

"Look, I know that jealousy crap is your jam, but it's not mine, bro. I don't know where she got the balls to think that was okay."

After pulling up to the curb outside the American Airlines departure doors, I looked over at my sister. "Ash, I don't expect you to understand, but I've been cracking away at her armor for months and finally got through it tonight. The way she freaked out was entirely uncalled for, but something happened this last weekend when she was back in New York, and instead of being there for her like I usually am, I was pretty harsh before I walked away."

"And you're probably going to go running back to her like the *pup* you are. Aren't you?" Ashlee asked as she opened her door to get out of my truck. "Does she know? About our parents and the fact that they left us everyth–"

"No, I haven't told her anything," I cut her off as I got out of the truck to grab her luggage from the backseat. I brought it around and pulled her into a hug. "I don't even know where to begin with that whole story. Regardless, I need a few days to get my head straight before I talk to her at all. Just promise you'll give her another chance when you meet her again?"

"I make no promises. Pretty disappointed, Tyler. Not gonna lie. Rylee was cool as shit. I was expecting the same from Sadie. Try to make it up to see me soon, okay?" She grabbed her backpack, swinging the strap over her shoulder as she started to wheel her luggage away.

"Miss you already!" I called after her.

"Miss you more!"

Once I saw her make it through the doors, I got back in my truck with every intention of going back to Sugar and Scotch. But as I drove away from the airport, I convinced myself to head home instead. Like I'd told my sister, I knew I needed space to clear my head.

"HEY, YOU'RE COMING TONIGHT, RIGHT?" Chance asked, interrupting my head math as he came into our office.

The numbers faded away as I blinked and rolled my eyes behind my glasses, tossing the notepad I was holding on my desk. "What's tonight?"

"What do you mean what's tonight?! It's game night at our house, man."

"Tonight is Thursday. Game nights are on Fridays."

It had been three and a half days since I'd left Sadie at Sugar and Scotch. I kept telling myself it wasn't any worse than her being in New York and ignoring my texts. But it had been agonizing not to talk to her, and she hadn't reached out to me either.

"We have George and Lynette coming into town, along with my parents, this weekend, remember?" Rylee's voice rang out.

My head swiveled to where she stood in the doorway, holding a box of what smelled like freshly baked peanut butter oatmeal cookies. I stood to grab the box from her after half a hug and a quick peck on the cheek.

"This is exactly the pick me up I needed." I moaned, biting into a cookie. "Also, I totally forgot the grandparents and parentals were coming into town this weekend."

"Give me one," Chance whined as he reached out from where he sat at his desk.

Clutching the box to my chest, I sat back down. "No way, man. You get this shit at home all the time. These are for me. Right, Ry?"

She laughed. "Well, technically, they're for all the guys, too. But he has a point, Chance. There is a fresh batch at home."

"So unfair!" he cried. I pulled out another cookie and leaned over to toss the box on his desk. We'd pushed our desks together to form an L-shape when we hired more guys and needed some extra space in our small office.

"Have you talked to Sadie? Is she coming tonight?" I tried to ask casually. Out of my peripheral, I could see Chance smirk as he shoved a cookie in his mouth, and I fought not to turn and glare at him.

Rylee smiled at me sadly and nodded her head. "She is. You should try and talk to her, Tyler. Let her explain everything. There's a lot you don't know that happened last weekend. And she feels awful for her outburst at the bar."

"How is she? Is she going back this weekend?" I started to click on random things on my computer so it didn't seem like I was too interested, but a quick glance at Rylee's upturned pink lips told me she wasn't buying my act.

"I don't think she's going back this weekend, but I'm not entirely sure. Maybe you guys could talk before you come over tonight?" she suggested.

I was torn between texting Sadie to ask if she wanted to have a drink beforehand so we *could* talk about what had happened on Sunday. Or wait until we had the presence of our friends to buffer what would be an inevitably uncomfortable conversation.

The ache in my chest from not talking to her for the past few days, for leaving her the way I did, gnawed away at me until I grabbed my phone and sent her a message before losing the nerve.

> Hey, I know it's been a few days, but would you maybe want to meet up for a drink before game night tonight?

"I gotta get back to the bakery. It was good to see you, Tyler. I'll see you guys later tonight." Rylee leaned over to kiss Chance goodbye. Her bright orange heels looked like she was wearing traffic cones on her feet, and I laughed as my phone vibrated in my hand.

The smile quickly vanished, and my heart dropped to my stomach as I read Sadie's reply.

> Already have plans. Wouldn't want you to have the sloppy second date of the night.

Fuck.

NOT GONNA LIE; I was kinda pissed. I grilled Chance for whatever information he had on Sadie's supposed *date*. And Rylee didn't answer us when we messaged her about it in a group chat with just the three of us.

My muscles were tight with tension as I pulled into Chance's driveway later that night, Sadie's car nowhere to be seen. It was bad enough I had to deal with the fact that she'd slept with her husband, but now she was out on a date with another man?

Chance and Rylee's house smelled like pot roast when I walked in and kicked off my shoes. Domino met me at the door, peering up at me like he expected to be petted, but I knew if I reached down, the little fucker would hiss and swipe at me with his paws of death. I don't know what I ever did to deserve his wrath, but that fluff ball really disliked me for some reason. And I swore he hadn't even been in the room when I'd told Chance I liked dogs more–back when he and I had first become friends.

"Hey, guys!" I announced myself before walking around the corner and into the kitchen because I didn't once, and I was now scarred for life at seeing Rylee spread eagle on the dining table, while Chance went down on her. Thank God they were facing the other way, so I didn't get a complete eyeful of Rylee's cookie, but I'd been traumatized all the same.

"Hey, Ty. Sorry for not responding earlier. We had an emergency at work. One of the bar sinks got clogged," Rylee explained as she hugged me.

"It's fine, but I still wanna know who she's on a date with," I said, walking over to where the open door led out to their patio. Chance was coming back from the swamp, which meant he either just forced Gary back to his home or went and fed him.

We'd watched *Lake Placid*, finally, and what did this dumbass do? He started to feed Gary.

Chance was convinced that if he only fed his *water puppy* things like fruit and veggies, the gator would eventually become a vegetarian.

I'd told him one day Gary would eat Domino because people get cranky when they go on diets. Why wouldn't gators?

"Who Sadie is on a date with?" Rylee's voice cut through my thoughts. "Why do you think Sadie is on a date? She's still at the bar with Javier trying to get the sink to work."

Chance came back into the house and patted my back as he walked by. "Hope you're hungry."

His words weren't lost on me, and my eye twitched. "So the sink thing ruined her date?"

Chance gave me a funny look as Rylee spun around and looked at me like I had just asked the dumbest question in the world. But I will die on the hill that there are no stupid questions, only stupid answers.

"There's no date. Sadie has not and will not go on a date. Did she tell you she was? And you believed her? God, you two are unbearable sometimes." She moved to pull what looked like rice pudding out of the oven as she spoke, so she missed the way my eyes narrowed at her as a grin spread across my face. Chance just shook his head at us both.

Sadie was a little liar. All to try and get under my skin. Did I deserve it? Yeah, what I had said hadn't been nice. And the last few days made me realize that she was probably tormenting herself over the situation with her husband.

They also made me realize that I hadn't been there for her. I was ashamed of that fact. I'd once told her I would always be there for her, no matter what. Yet, I acted like a jerk when it mattered most. She had every right to be angry with me.

The sound of the door opening and closing caught my ear. "Something smells good! I'm starving," Sadie's voice rang out.

Tension bled from my body at the sound of her voice, and for a moment, everything just felt right. Like there was no drama in the happy little family we'd all created. But as she rounded the corner and caught my eye, I was quickly reminded that wasn't the case.

Her smile dropped, and a calm expression took over her beautiful face as she looked at me. For a moment, it was as if Chance, Rylee, and everything else disappeared. It was just me and Sadie, and all the feelings and thoughts we'd never said out loud filled the space between us like a pot about to boil over.

"How was your date?" I asked.

She blinked, our moment broken by my stupid fucking question—okay, I guess there *are* some stupid questions, and everything else rushed back into the picture. Chance murmured to Rylee over her shoulder, their whispered words not loud enough for me to hear as they ignored us.

"I'm sure you know there was no date, Tyler," Sadie said as she started to make herself a martini. Chance already spread out all the ingredients to our drinks of choice for our game night ritual. Sadie with her martini, Rylee with her rosé, while he and I usually drank a few beers or sipped on whiskey.

I looked back at our friends. Rylee was making a not-so-subtle head movement in an attempt to get me to go over and talk to her best friend. Not that I wanted to have this conversation in front of them, but knowing it was me who put the unhappy look on Sadie's face was more than enough for me to suck up my pride.

Approaching her, I bumped her shoulder gently with mine. "Hey, do you want to go talk out on the patio?"

She shook her head slightly as she popped an olive in her mouth. "Now isn't the time, Pup."

Well, at least she called me Pup.

"I don't think they're gonna mind if we step out for a few moments," I argued, reaching for her glass so she'd have to follow me.

Her reflexes were quicker than I'd anticipated, though, as her hand shot out and slapped mine away from her drink. "I don't *want* to talk right now."

She moved away to talk to Rylee as Chance came to stand beside me. "Want me to sic Gary on her so you can be her knight in shining armor?"

Laughing, I poured myself a small glass of Glen-fiddich. "I think we both know it would more than likely be *her* that saved *me* from Gary."

We started to bring stuff to the table. Our usual ritual consisted of eating dinner together there, before we moved to the living room to play one of the random games Chance and I had accrued over the last few years. We tended to lean toward games with trivia, where we could be in teams, and currently, the group's favorite had been The Blockbuster Game.

Chance and Rylee took their usual seats on one side of the six-person table while I took mine. It was a few moments before I realized Sadie hadn't sat next to me but was taking her time preparing another drink as if she were trying to delay being near me. When she finally sat down, I breathed a small sigh of relief that she hadn't tried to sit at the head of the table next to Rylee, and I deliberately scooted my seat a little closer to hers.

"Was Javier able to figure the sink out?" Rylee asked Sadie as she placed some salad on her plate.

"Yeah, we have no idea what clogged it or what the problem was, but it's all figured out now. I didn't wanna leave Riya to deal with it. That's why I waited until it was finished," Sadie answered as she served herself.

I noticed she only put one piece of potato, three carrots, and a small piece of meat on her plate and filled the rest with salad. She always ate like a mouse when she came back from New York. It usually would take her a few days until she'd start eating differently again, and I hated that it was like that.

Once she'd warmed up to me and we had actually started to get to know one another, I noticed that New York Sadie and Jacksonville Sadie were almost two totally different people. It was so clear how her life there made her miserable. But she insisted that there was still a part of her that loved the city and who she was while she was there.

And it often made me wonder which one was the real Sadie Tailor.

I widened my legs as I ate, and my foot found

hers under the table. I'd done it a million times before, and Sadie would normally play footsies with me throughout dinner, but tonight she shuffled her foot away as she continued her conversation with Rylee.

Chance caught my eye across the table and gave a slight nod toward Sadie as he asked quietly, "You okay, Ty?"

Nodding, I picked at my food, my appetite suddenly gone. We all made small talk through the rest of dinner. Sadie kept giving me short, clipped answers whenever I'd try and ask her a question, and my anger started to seep back in as the night continued.

"If you guys will excuse us for just a moment, we need to go put out our nightly offerings for Gary. We'll be right back. Go set the game up in the living room," Chance said, giving me a sly wink as he and I finished cleaning the dishes.

Sadie and Rylee had been whispering on the couch in the living room. Sadie's back was to the kitchen, so when Chance and Rylee disappeared out the patio doors, she didn't know it as I came up behind her.

"Can we talk now?" I asked as my lips brushed her ear and caused her to jump.

"Jesus, Tyler. No, I'm not going to have this conversation with you here. Just drop it already," she spoke without looking at me, her voice laced with aggravation.

I sat in the space Rylee had occupied a few moments earlier and faced Sadie as my knees bumped hers. Reaching for her chin to stop her from looking away, I spoke calmly, "I'm sorry for what I said. It was a complete dick thing to do, and I regret my word choice."

She jerked her chin away and glared at me. "It doesn't matter if you're sorry, Tyler. All you did was prove that you're no different than any other man. The minute you found out someone touched your shiny toy, you threw it away because you didn't want it anymore." Her voice cracked at the end, and I felt that crack in my chest.

Sadie had once admitted that she felt safe with me. And I felt like I'd taken that trust she'd learned to have in me and thrown it out the window. I'd been a typical asshole, just like she said. And it pained me to think that perhaps...

"You acted no better than Scott would have," she finished my internal thought for me, and my heart dropped into my stomach.

"Sadie–"

"Can we please just *not* tonight?" She sounded tired. Tired of the drama, tired of the shit the men in her life put her through, tired of dealing with everything that she shouldered with so much grace.

I remained silent as she moved from the couch we were on to the opposite one. Neither of us spoke, and when Chance and Rylee came back, Sadie's demeanor instantly changed, and the three of them decided it would be a guys-against-girls night. My heart wasn't in it as the evening wound on. And I knew her well enough to know that Sadie was putting on a show as she pretended she was having a good time while ignoring me.

I felt like the proverbial puppy who'd lashed out at its owner and been put in the kennel for a time-out, while the other animals still got to play.

Eventually, when the night was over, for the first time in a long time, I was glad to be going home to be by myself. But it seemed as if fate had other plans. Sadie and I had said goodnight to our friends at the same time and walked out together after an awkward and barely audible farewell on her part. And since she was parked behind me, I had to wait for her to leave before I could get out of the driveway.

But for some reason, her car wouldn't start.

When I realized this, I sat in my truck with a giant grin. There was no way there was anything wrong with her car. Sadie took better care of that car than most people did their kids. I felt like it had something to do with Chance and Rylee's *offering* to Gary earlier in the evening.

"Need a ride?" I asked out my open window, after she got back out while letting out a string of curses.

"No, I'll ask Rylee," she answered as she started back toward the house.

"Come on, Wifey. Don't make her take you home if I'm offering."

After a sigh on her part, and a quiet chuckle on mine, she grabbed her purse from her car and got in my passenger seat. I didn't say anything as she buckled herself in while I went about making an eight-point turn to get my truck out of the driveway.

"So, will you talk to me now?" I asked as we pulled onto the main road.

"I have nothing to say to you right now, Tyler. I'm upset. With myself, with Scott, with you. Everything just fucking sucks right now, and I don't want to talk about it," she answered as she stared out the window.

"Will you just tell me what happened? If anything, just tell me that. You always talk to me, and I know I made you feel like you couldn't, and I'm sorry for that. I was angry. Not even about the fact that you slept with him, Sadie, it was because he constantly sleeps around on you, and you let *him* take care of your needs, rather than just giving in to this insane attraction we have for each other."

She threw her hands up and turned to look at me. "Jesus Christ, okay, I guess we're doing this then. Yes, I let him take care of my needs. Because he surprised me by showing up when he wasn't supposed to be there, and he caught me *giggling* at the photo you sent me of your dick! So, yes, I placated him to distract him from the fact that he caught me having a moment over another man's cock.

"And while I was appeasing him, he somehow

convinced me he wasn't cheating on me. And that everything that's been printed in the last year has been a lie. Then he left me alone all afternoon for work like he always does and came home to put a collar of diamonds around my neck. A big, beautiful, fucking Harry Winston metaphor to remind me that he *owns* me.

"So, yes, I let him fuck me. Or rather, I fucked him. Multiple times, as a matter of fact, only to find out that he'd been lying about everything and that, once again, I was a fucking fool."

"I don't need to hear about how many times you fucked him, Sadie," I growled through clenched teeth and gripped the steering wheel tighter. I felt as angry as she looked, and she snarled at me as she continued, like I hadn't said anything at all.

"Because I let myself fucking fall for his charms even though I *knew* better! And the worst part is I thought of *you* the entire time, and it made me feel like I was a bad wife! But it put everything into perspective for me when I found that stupid card, and found out about his stupid secret, and I rushed back here because I wanted to be with *you*! And then I saw you with your fucking sister, and I just saw red and had no control over myself, which isn't *me*! I don't act irrationally. Everything I do is with purpose. And I agonized over whether or not I was ready to be with you, and I was, and now I fucking hate that I feel like I don't know anything!"

Some of my anger subsided with her confession.

"You're not a bad wife, Sadie. And I'm sorry I sent you the picture. I shouldn't have. I just thought we'd finally reached this place where, maybe, we could stop playing this game with each other. As for my sister, well, maybe that's the hint you needed to *admit* you want me just as badly as I want you."

"It was never a question of whether or not I want you, Tyler. It was whether or not I would consciously decide to be a cheater just because my husband was."

I pulled into the parking lot for her condo. The drive had been short since we all lived less than ten minutes away from each other. She made a noise of protest as I turned my vehicle off, and I told her, "I'm gonna walk you up. At least give me peace of mind to know you made it in safely."

It was a shit excuse to go upstairs with her, and we both knew it, but she allowed it and led the way. I'd only been to her condo a few times before. Usually, everything we did was either at mine or Chance's house, but it still felt like home as she opened the door, and I was welcomed by the spicy vanilla scent that was purely *Sadie*.

"Okay, I made it safe. You can go now," she grumbled as she tossed her purse on the table in the small entry hall and swung the door back in my face.

Before it could shut all the way, I grabbed the frame and pushed it open again. She whirled around and glared as I stepped in and slammed the door behind me. "What are you doing?"

Advancing on her quickly, she retreated until her back hit the wall next to the hallway opening that led to her bedroom. I didn't stop until we were nearly chest-to-chest. "So, what was your decision?"

Her brows furrowed as she stared at me in confusion. "What?"

Lifting my arms, I caged her against the wall just like I'd done at her office. Confusion melted into desire as I repeated my words in a husky whisper. "Did you decide to say fuck you to your husband and give in to this? Give in to us?"

A multitude of emotions played out on her face as she stared at me. Our chests rose and fell in tandem with our heavy, bated breaths. My hands fell away from the wall, as one found its way to her hip while I cradled her face in the palm of the other, my thumb sweeping lazy strokes against her cheekbone.

I rested my forehead against hers, and her eyes fluttered closed as I whispered, "Tell me all you want is for us to be friends, and I will walk out that door right now and never push you for more again. I hope to God that isn't the case, though, because all I want to do is fucking worship you for hours. But if you want me to stop, then I will settle for continuing to worship the ground you walk on."

She sucked in a breath as her eyes opened. My eyes dropped to her lips as they pulled into a conquered smile. "I have never wanted something, or someone, as badly as I want you, Tyler Michaelson, and I am tired of trying to resist it," she whispered.

Relief flooded my veins, followed quickly by the craving I'd never felt for another woman–only her. Somewhere in the back of my mind, I knew this would be the beginning of the end. Deep down, there was a small thread that tethered me to the thought that this would end badly for both of us.

And I snapped that thread just as quickly as my self-restraint.

OUR FIRST REAL KISS WASN'T SOFT OR SWEET. Our lips collided, and our tongues tangled in an explosion of heat and passion. My hands knotted in his hair as he lifted me against the wall, and my legs wrapped around his waist. Tyler kissed me so deeply, that I didn't know where he ended, and I began.

Arousal gathered between my legs as he rocked against me. Then, with a tight grip on my ass, he pulled me away from the wall and started toward my couch. His lips moved to my neck as he set me down gently, teeth skimming my sensitive skin, before he pulled back to look at me despite my noise of protest.

Barely a second went by before I reached out and grabbed him by his shirt, hauling him back to me before my fingers found the button and zipper of his pants. "I need you, Tyler. Now."

"Fuck, Sadie," he groaned, kissing me again as I shoved his pants down. He reached for the hem of my shirt and pulled it over my head, breaking our kiss once more. Standing, I removed his shirt while he stepped out of his pants, then made quick work of my shorts and underwear while he dug into the pocket of his jeans to grab his wallet.

My mouth salivated at the sight of his cock, standing at attention and peeking out of the top of his boxer briefs. The real-life thing was *much* better than a photo. "Fuck, I can't wait to have that in me."

He chuckled lowly as he dropped his wallet and ripped open the wrapper of a condom. My labs had all come back clean—thank God—but better safe than sorry. I watched as he pushed his boxers down and rolled the condom over his cock.

Licking my lips, I told him, "I don't know if you're going to fit."

My fingers ghosted down my stomach, ready to relieve some of the pressure between my legs, when he caught my hand in his own. The fingers of his other hand continued the journey I'd started, until they were sliding through my center and up to circle my clit gently. "You're going to take every inch of me," he whispered against my lips as I threw my head back and gasped.

His fingers slid through my arousal again before they teased my entrance, and he pushed two inside me. My hands found his shoulders as my hips rocked against him, desperate to feel more. He continued to pump his fingers into me while he reached around with his other hand and unsnapped my bra. I shrugged out of it as his eyes moved to my naked breasts.

"God, you're fucking beautiful," he murmured, palming one in his hand. He leaned down to bite my nipple as he pushed a third finger into me.

Crying out, my hands found the back of his head as I pushed my chest into his face, and his teeth clamped down harder. I could feel how wet I was as a spike of pain shot through me before it was replaced with a wave of pleasure. My orgasm was nearing as Tyler's teeth let up, and he sucked on my nipple while his tongue soothed it. His fingers started to move faster, his thumb finding my clit, and he let go of my breast with a pop of his mouth.

"Come for me, Sadie. Let me feel how ready that pussy is for my cock."

His words sent me over the edge, and I saw stars as I came around his fingers with a hoarse moan. Tyler's lips found mine, and he swallowed my cries as he pulled his fingers out of me and turned us. He gripped my hips as he sat on the couch and pulled me down to straddle him. His dick was rock solid, bulging against the condom as it lay long and thick against his stomach.

Guiding me to my knees with one hand, he gripped himself in the other and slid his cock against the cum that coated my thighs. "Sink onto me slowly. I want to savor watching you take me inch by inch."

Biting my lip, I started to lower myself, relishing the look that crossed his face as my pussy began to swallow him. My body tingled with pure ecstasy as he stretched me, slowly, until I felt like he would rip me in half if I kept going.

I started to push back up onto my knees, but he stopped me by gripping my hips harder. He shook his head as his eyes moved from where we were joined together to meet mine, half-lidded and shining with unadulterated lust. "You want to know how I know you can take all of me?" he asked, his voice low and gravelly.

I stared at him in awe as he slowly pushed his hips up and dragged me back down onto him. My breathing was shallow as a hint of pain spread low in my abdomen. It must have shown on my face because he reached between us and started to rub my clit in lazy strokes, and the pain quickly diminished.

"How?" I threw my head back and closed my eyes, focusing on the immense pleasure that started to build. My voice was laced with need as my hips started to rock in sync with his fingers.

A few moments later, we sucked in a breath simultaneously, and my eyes flew open as I realized I was fully seated on him. My hips stilled as my hands planted on his chest, and we stared at each other, neither of us moving, before he said, "Because you were fucking made for *me*. You were always meant to be *mine*."

Our mouths collided again as I started to move against him. He thrust up as I rocked forward, the tip of him bumping my cervix. I'd imagined it would be painful, but I liked the faint shock of pain paired with the pleasure. Tyler continued to work my clit as our kiss broke, and we both looked down at where we were joined.

The familiar pressure began to build again, and I leaned back as my hips worked faster. "Tyler, I'm going to come."

"Yeah, baby? Let me feel that pussy milk my cock." He started to thrust into me faster and worked my clit harder. "Fuck, I'm going to come, too."

I cried out as I came, and he followed me a second later, wrapping his arms around my back and pulling me to his chest. He sank his teeth into the skin where my shoulder met my neck, and I could feel his cock twitch inside me as he came with a roar against my skin.

Our breathing was in sync as we rode out our climaxes. I dropped my head to his shoulder and vaguely registered Tyler's teeth, releasing my skin before his tongue soothed the sting. "Did I hurt you?" he whispered against me.

Shaking my head, I moved to get off his lap. "No, but I'm sure I'll feel it in the morning. Your dick is like a gift from the gods. Amazing, but it comes with a price," I joked.

I rubbed my abdomen as he slipped out of me and rose to my feet as I watched him take the condom off. With how full it looked, I was surprised the damn thing didn't break.

"I'm serious, Sadie. Are you okay?" He looked at me with concern as he got off the couch to throw the condom away.

Maybe it was the tone of his voice, but something told me this had been a problem with women in his past. I followed him into the kitchen, our naked bodies glistening with sweat, as I grabbed two glasses and filled them with water. Before offering one to him, I kissed him gently and ran my other hand through his hair. "I'm fine. I promise. It's gonna take more than your massive cock to hurt me. Trust me."

Pulling back with a smirk, I sipped my water, and his lips turned up in a grin after gulping down his glass. "Is that permission to be a little rougher with you, Wifey?"

Tyler pulled me to him again and kissed me hard, our tongues tangling together. His cock stirred between us, and my nipples hardened as my body grew ready to take him again. Tyler had said I was made for him, and I believed it as my body tingled in anticipation of him being rougher with me.

"Permission granted, Pup," I spoke against his lips.

A surprised squeal left my lips as he scooped me, bridal style, in his arms and rushed down the hall toward my bedroom. I laughed as he tossed me on my bed and started to crawl after me before jumping back up quickly. "Fuck. Hold on."

He hurried out of my room, and I admired the muscles of his well-sculpted body as he went.

Moments later, he appeared with what looked like a handful of condoms. "Did you have all of those in your wallet?" I laughed.

"I've been carrying them since the first night I met you." He set them on the nightstand next to my bed before he crawled on and kissed me.

"Mmm, someone was eager," I whispered breathlessly between kisses. My legs came up to press on either side of his hips as I urged him closer to me. I could feel his cock slide against my center, and I bit his lower lip between my teeth while rocking against him.

Sucking in a breath, he pulled back, his lip stretching between us before I let it go. He quickly flipped me onto my stomach and smacked a hand against my ass. Yelping, I arched my back as he reached for another condom. I started to rise to my knees, but he pushed me back down, and I felt his weight settle on my back as his cock nudged against my entrance.

"Fucking hopeful," he growled into my ear as he slowly pushed inside me. My hips raised slightly. One of his hands slipped under them, and his fingers found my clit, working it as he thrust into me.

He pressed me into the bed, and my arms lay out in front of me, hands gripping the sheets as he slowly moved. His other hand stretched out and reached for mine as he nuzzled my neck from behind. I could feel the hard muscles of his body tense against me with every unhurried stroke.

"You feel so fucking good, taking my cock so well," he whispered into my ear, earning a low moan from me.

He didn't lay his whole weight against me so that he could work my clit with his fingers. As my hips gently rocked forward into his hand, I squeezed my inner walls around his cock.

"Fuuuck, Sadie. Do that again," he commanded.

I readily complied as he skimmed his teeth down the back of my neck. His hips started to move faster, snapping into my backside. "You like taking directions, don't you? Do you like being a good girl, Sadie?"

Fuck, yes. I was a very dominant woman in most aspects of my life. But it was my little secret that I liked being told what to do in the bedroom. It had been part of the reason I enjoyed my choker of diamonds so much. The meaning behind them when I wore them during sex.

Nodding, I turned my head to the side. "Yes, I like being your good girl, Tyler."

"Fucking right, you do. Now, I want to hear you when you come. Get loud for me, baby." He dropped his full weight onto my back, angling his hips to get as deep as possible as he removed his fingers from my clit.

Tyler didn't know it, but this was my favorite way to be fucked.

The position made me feel so impossibly full, and his hands clenched around mine as he rode me into the bed. With every thrust, I rewarded him with a raspy, needy cry, earning a groan of satisfaction from him in return. Even though he was heavy, I didn't care. The friction caused my clit to rub against the silk of my duvet, creating another swirling sensation to add to the long list of things I already felt.

My body wasn't sure *what* it was supposed to feel as I struggled to breathe yet continued chasing my climax. Tyler tensed above me, and I knew he was close, so I squeezed my inner walls hard as he drove into me deeper, and the motion caused us both to come together. I let out a high-pitched moan as he groaned loudly into my ear.

Immediately after, he shifted off me to his side, gathering me in his arms and pulling me till my back rested against his chest. "Are you okay?"

I breathed heavily, my vision spotty from the lack of air, as I sucked huge gulps of it into my lungs. "Mmhmm."

He kissed the top of my head, having shifted us so that I was tucked under his chin, and his other hand moved in soft patterns against the skin of my abdomen.

My hands reached up to grip his arm that held me around my shoulders. I leaned back a little, looking over my shoulder at him. "You don't have to ask me every time. I promise I won't break."

Tyler leaned down and kissed me softly before he pushed my sweaty hair off my forehead. "I will always make sure I'm not hurting you."

"I'll tell you, okay? Besides, you like it when I'm loud." I cocked my eyebrow and smirked up at him.

Laughing, he nudged me back, setting his chin on my head. "I do like telling you what to do. I have a feeling this is the only time you'll let me," he spoke sleepily.

His soft breathing evened out, and I had a feeling he'd fallen asleep, so I snuggled deeper into him, satiated and content, and let sleep take hold of me as well.

MY BODY WAS DELICIOUSLY SORE when I woke up the following day. It was barely light outside, and I glanced at my clock that hung on the wall to see that it was six forty-five. Stretching out underneath my sheet, I smiled and turned to snuggle into Tyler.

Only he wasn't there.

A sudden pang of disappointment shot through me as I sat up, clutching the sheet to my chest as I looked around for him. Getting out of bed, I slipped into my black silk robe. Tyler's shoes were still in the entryway, and his clothes were still piled by the couch.

Frowning, I called out, "Tyler?"

The morning breeze fluttered the curtains in the living room, drawing my attention to the fact that the sliding door that led to my balcony was open.

Clutching my robe tighter, I stepped out, squinting to see beyond the empty patio. The sun hadn't started to rise just yet, the light low and hazy.

Movement pulled my attention down to the beach to see a dark spot against the sand near where the waves broke at the shoreline. I descended the stairs that led from my condo to the beach below, realizing that Tyler was swimming out in the ocean and was on his way back to the shore.

Chuckling, I crossed my arms and walked further onto the beach. The morning air was muggy but slightly cool against my skin. As I neared the dark blob I'd seen from the balcony, I realized it was Tyler's underwear on one of my beach towels.

As he emerged from the water, completely naked, I yelled out, "Tyler, what are you doing?"

"Hush! The show was just getting good!" A raspy voice sounded behind me. I jumped and whirled around. On the patio that belonged to the condo below me, there was an elderly lady sitting at a table. She had a cup of coffee before her, and a bowl of mixed fruit sat beside a pair of binoculars. Her cotton candy pink hair was wild and curly, and she wore a pair of neon pink glasses attached to a large, beaded necklace.

"Let an old lady die happy, would you? I was just looking for dolphins, but this was much better." She motioned to the binoculars. "I didn't even need these. Good for you, sweetheart."

Laughing, I shook my head and turned back to

where Tyler was now completely exposed as he walked toward me. He smiled as he leaned down to pick up his boxers. "Good morning, Wifey."

"Oh, it's a good morning, alright. You gave the lady who lives below me quite the show," I explained and pointed over my shoulder.

Tyler peeked behind me and waved, completely unashamed, as he yelled, "Good morning!"

"It certainly was!" she called back.

We laughed on our way back up the stairs, and as soon as the door slid shut behind him, I launched myself into his arms and kissed him. "I'm not going to lie; I felt a little rejected when I woke up, and you weren't there," I said after I pulled back.

"I'm sorry, Wifey. I take a swim every morning. It's just a habit. I certainly didn't think anyone would be awake to see me in all my naked glory. And I didn't think you'd be awake yet." He chuckled as he wrapped his arms around me and kissed the tip of my nose.

"As much as I want you again, let me shower first. Unless you want to join me?" he suggested with a waggle of his brows.

Warmth exploded between my thighs at his words, and I opened my mouth to tell him that, of course, I wanted to shower with him. But my confession was interrupted by a knock on the door.

We both froze at the intrusion before Tyler's eyes turned to the door. "Are you expecting someone?"

Shaking my head, I whispered, "No. Maybe it's just Rylee and Chance?"

The actuality of it being Scott loomed over us as I headed to the door and peered out the peephole. Sighing in relief, I moved to open it. "It's just a package."

Tyler's shoulders visibly sagged as I signed for the black box tied with a red satin ribbon. A card was slipped into the bow on the top, and I just knew it was from Scott. Placing the box on the breakfast bar, I walked back to Tyler. "Now, how about that shower?"

"What's with the box?" he asked, ignoring my question as he jerked his head toward the offending parcel.

I sighed. "It's got pretty wrapping and a big bow. It's probably from Scott. I'm supposed to go back there next weekend."

Tyler let out a low growl as he walked around me and grabbed the card from the top. "I expect you to be wearing this with your diamonds when I get home next Friday," he read.

Shame coursed through me, but not from the fact that I'd cheated on my husband. It was from Tyler having to read Scott's words. Tyler crumpled the card in his hand and ripped the ribbon off the box, opening it to peer inside, snorting as he pulled lingerie out of the satin-lined container.

It was a black underbust corset that tied in the back, with garters hanging from it. He reached in and picked up a black matching G-string before his eyes found mine. "There are even matching stockings. He really likes dressing up his doll, doesn't he?"

He dropped the outfit back into the box and stormed past me, moving down the hall. Turning, I called out to him, "Tyler, you can't be mad. It's not like I knew he was going to send this."

He didn't stop as he replied, "Not mad at you, Wifey. Just irritated at that prick who thinks he fucking owns you."

The door to the bathroom shut, and the shower water turned on a few seconds later. Sighing, I walked over to admire the lingerie. It was actually quite flattering and something that would have looked amazing with my diamonds. Scott always did have excellent taste.

My phone dinged, and I saw that he had messaged me as if the devil himself had been summoned by my mere thoughts.

Did you get your gift?

I did. Unfortunately, I won't be able to make it back next weekend. Gotta train the new girl.

You need to stay all weekend for that?

Riya didn't need to be trained at all, but he didn't need to know that. I picked the corset up again as he sent another message.

Snorting, I looked over my shoulder down the hall. An idea formed. I smirked and gathered the contents of the box.

My phone vibrated again before I could set it down, but I ignored it and left it on the breakfast bar, before making my way down the hall. I quickly got out of my robe and slipped into the lingerie. I'd worn so many pieces between modeling and wearing it for Scott that I was able to tie and secure myself in quickly, finishing just as I heard the water turn off in the bathroom.

My choker had been left in New York because I had no need for it down here. But I had a more petite choker-style necklace made of two strings of pearls with cushion-cut, dark-colored sapphires between them. It was the perfect statement piece. I finished closing the clasp on it and draped myself on the bed on my side just as Tyler came out of the bathroom.

He stopped when he saw me, water still dripping down his abs as he swore. "Fuck, Sadie. No way in hell is Scott fucking seeing you in that."

I slowly stretched out until I was flat on my back, maintaining eye contact with him. His eyes darted down to my necklace, and I reached up and fingered a sapphire, while arching my back and pushing my bare breasts in the air. "I got it for myself because it reminded me of your eyes."

He gulped, his throat bobbing as he dropped the towel that was wrapped around his waist. His cock was already hard and ready for me, with a drop of precum beaded at his slit. "What am I going to fucking do with you?"

I licked my lips as he kneeled on the bed and straddled my waist, resting his weight on his fists as he looked down at me. I reached up to cup his cheek in one hand, while wrapping the other around his shaft. My thumb swiped over his head, spreading that bead of desire as his eyes fluttered closed.

Pulling his head down gently until my lips rested against his ear, I started to stroke him and whispered, "I'm *yours* now, Tyler. You get to do whatever you want with me."

CHAPTER ELEVEN

Tyler

Fucking Sadie was my new favorite hobby.

Next week, I'd turn twenty-seven, but I felt like my birthday wish had come true every time I came inside her. Granted, we'd only been fucking for the past thirty-six hours, but I had no plans on stopping our coital activities any time soon.

I was in trouble.

I'd been obsessed with her for the last six and a half months, but now that she was *mine,* I was fucking strung out on the liquid drug between her legs.

But she wasn't really mine. And I thought it would be easy to live with our situation.

However, it hadn't even been two days, and I knew if I tried to quit her cold turkey, I'd die from withdrawals. I'd told her it could be our little secret, and I'd told myself I could be whatever she needed me to be. But now that I knew what she felt like, what she tasted like, it made my blood boil to think about her returning to New York, so that her sorry excuse for a husband could put his hands on her.

"Are you going to get to work, Pup? Or are you going to just stand there while I do everything?" her teasing lilt cut through my thoughts.

My gaze cleared as my eyes found hers. She was smiling at me while she spread pink and white rose petals along the top of the bar. Returning her smile, I continued setting up candles on the floor and placing them between the petals. "Why isn't Chance doing this again?"

"Because the only thing that would keep Rylee from the bakery today was his magical penis. If I'd asked her to have a girls' day, she would have wanted to come by at some point to do something work-related," she answered.

Rylee's parents and Chance's grandparents had to leave town because Lynette wasn't feeling well and they'd driven together, or so they'd told Rylee. They were waiting for that evening to show back up at the bakery, when Chance proposed, to surprise her.

I set the box of candles down and walked around the bar to stand behind her. "Do you think my penis is magical?" My hands found her waist, and I nuzzled her neck as she laughed softly.

Sadie spun around and wrapped her arms around my neck. "Your penis is the *most* magical. It's so magical, as a matter of fact, that it has somehow managed to make all those condoms you had disappear. So no more playtime until you pick up more."

"Aww but, Wifey, if it's so magical, can't it just magically vanish any baby makers before they swim to their destination?" I asked before kissing her lightly. Her spicy vanilla scent, mixed with the sweet aroma of the baked goods, was doing things to my body, and I was tempted to sit her on the bar top and bury my face between her thighs.

She giggled. The first time I heard her giggle, I decided that it was my favorite sound in the world and that I would spend as much time as possible drawing it from her lips. One of her hands moved to clutch the hair at the back of my head, and she gripped it hard, pulling me in to kiss me.

Her lips were plump and swollen with as much as I'd bitten them in the last day and a half. Her tongue moved against mine in slow, unhurried strokes, and my dick stirred. My fingers found the button of her pants just as she broke our kiss and moved away from me.

"Nuh-uh, Pup. We have to finish setting this up. And you need to go buy more kitten mittens," she exclaimed with a wink.

I laughed and scrunched my nose at her. "Kitten mittens? Cute."

Laughing, she grabbed another handful of petals from the big box on the counter behind the bar and set about arranging a giant heart on the floor just inside the entrance. "You know, there isn't much left to do if you want to run to the store. I can meet you at your place in an hour? We'll have some time to kill before we need to be back to film this for her Claire and Collin."

"You sure there's nothing else I can do?" I asked. But she looked so focused on constructing the petals in a perfect heart shape, that I already knew she'd want to do the rest on her own. She was particular about decorations.

"I'm all good here. I'll see you in a little bit." She paused and looked over her shoulder, pursing her lips for a kiss.

A giddy feeling shot through me at how easily she showed affection, and I reached down to cradle her face, giving her a gentle kiss. The smile I was rewarded with stole my breath, and I silently cursed how far I'd fallen for this woman I couldn't fully claim as my own.

SADIE TOOK LONGER than we'd anticipated, so I caught up on a book while I waited. I'd changed into more comfortable clothes to lounge around in—sweats and a thin hoodie. The hood was pulled over my head as I burrowed into the plush black leather of my couch, stretched out and insanely comfortable.

I must have fallen asleep because I woke to Sadie's soft laughter as she pulled the book off my face. "You feeling okay, Pup?"

A lazy smile pulled my lips up, and I reached out for her. "Yeah, I guess I just needed a nap. Come here."

Pulling her down so she was straddling my stomach, I propped my legs up so she could rest against my thighs. "Did you get everything finished?"

"I did. And I would like to point out that this is an extremely awkward position, considering I am wearing a dress." She squirmed and pushed back to try to maneuver the short skirt of her flowy, navy dress down since it had bunched at her waist.

A husky chuckle left my mouth as I grabbed the back of her thighs and scooted her up my chest abruptly. I'd already been lying on one of the decorative pillows that came with the couch, so the movement allowed me to have a direct line of sight of the material that hid her perfect, pink pussy.

"Tyler! What are you doing?" she squealed.

"Staring at the light at the end of the tunnel," I murmured, running my thumb over her center. She wore a thin pair of silk bikini-style underwear, and I could feel she was already wet through them.

"Oh yeah? You think you're about to die?" She laughed as she spread her legs a little wider and lifted her hips, helping me remove her panties one leg at a time.

"Wifey, if I died right now, I would die a happy man."

She rested her elbows against my thighs and propped herself back up to look at me with a smirk.

Grabbing her hips, I shifted myself down and pulled her to her knees, so she hovered over my face, relishing how she bit her lip as she stared down at me.

Her skirt stayed bunched in my hands as I eased her down, not breaking eye contact as I stuck my tongue out to lick along her slick center. She moaned and threw her head back, so I pinched the skin of her butt where her skirt was gathered. "Keep your eyes on me while I fuck this slice of heaven with my tongue."

Sadie giggled as she looked back down at me through hooded eyes. She reached out to tangle one hand in my hair and braced the other on the back of the couch as I ran my tongue against her again.

I kissed her pussy like I kissed her mouth. Open, hot, and wet. My teeth scraped against her clit gently, before I plunged my tongue into her and she sucked in a breath as her hips started to move against my face.

"That's right, baby. I want you to drown me when you come," I urged, sucking her clit into my mouth.

"Oh my God, Tyler. Fuck!" she swore as she started to ride my face. My hands tightened around her backside and pulled her down, so she rested her weight fully on me.

"I don't want to hurt you," she whimpered as she tried to shift her weight back. But I curled my arms around the back of her thighs, so that my fists could lock against the front of her hip bones and hold her to me, as I continued to work her with my tongue.

Her breathy moans turned into hoarse cries as I alternated between fucking her with my tongue and sucking on her clit. My cock was so hard from the sounds she was making, that I thought I might explode if she simply touched it. Working my jaw faster, I rolled my tongue against her and suctioned my mouth to her sensitive bundle of nerves.

"Tyler, I'm going to come," she cried out as she gripped my hair harder.

Nodding my head against her, our eyes stayed connected as she came with a cry that was like music to my ears. I lapped up her release as she slowly rode my face until she was spent. Then, when she collapsed back against my legs, I kissed her inner thigh.

"I think I'm the one who died and went to heaven," she whispered contentedly.

A triumphant smile pulled my lips into a grin, but before I could say anything, she shifted off my legs and grabbed my hand to pull me up from the couch. "Your turn," she sang, leading me down the hall to my bedroom.

"Sadie, you don't have to. I know it's not easy," I told her.

Over the last day and a half, she'd tried to take all of me in her mouth—fuck had she tried—but my size made it difficult. She smiled back at me as we crossed the threshold. When we got to the edge of my bed, she let go of my hand and pulled my sweats down in one swoop, and my cock sprang free and bobbed in front of her.

She licked her lips before licking up the length of my shaft, causing me to suck in a sharp breath. Then she rose and pulled my hoodie over my head before quickly pulling her dress over hers, leaving her in just her bra as she crawled onto my bed.

Swallowing thickly, I watched as she positioned herself so that she was lying on her back with her head hanging slightly over the side as she stared upside down at me. "I looked it up, and this position is supposed to make it easier to deep-throat cocks your size."

I blinked at the normalcy with which she stated this information. And then again, at the fact that no woman I'd ever been with had taken the time to research how they could get better at sucking dick for *my* pleasure. "I hit the fucking jackpot with you," I whispered in awe.

She grinned, reaching her hands over her head toward me. I stepped into her arms, and her hands settled on my thighs as I gripped my cock and ran the head against her lips. She opened her mouth, and her tongue darted out to lick the length again, before she moved her head to the side to place open-mouth kisses on her way back up to the crown.

Leaning forward, I bent my knees slightly before sliding into her mouth. We worked together slowly, and I pulled back every so often, so that her spit could coat my cock before pushing forward again. It was the sexiest thing I'd ever seen or done with a woman before, and I wished I'd taken off her bra to see her glorious tits bouncing as she deep-throated me.

After a few slow thrusts, I groaned as she took the last inch of me in her mouth. Pausing, just holding myself there, I lightly fingered her throat as it bulged out from where my cock nestled inside it. "This is seriously the hottest fucking thing ever, Sadie."

The little minx grinned around my dick and made a hum of satisfaction that caused vibrations to run down my shaft, straight to my balls. "Fuck, I don't think I'm going to last."

She started to bob, and my head fell back as I slowly fucked her face, trying to keep my concentration. The wet sucking sounds were like ASMR to my fucking ears, and I knew I wouldn't last long like this.

Looking back down, I saw her eyes were closed as she greedily took my cock. Her thighs rubbed together, and I leaned over a little to reach between her legs. She moaned against me as my fingers found her clit, and one of her hands moved from my thigh to cup my balls, massaging them gently in her palm.

"Fuck, Sadie, I'm about to come." Her hips gently rocked against my hand as I rubbed her faster and looked down to see her nod as her grip tightened on me. My thrusts became erratic, and my breathing shallowed as I watched my cock move in and out of her mouth.

My balls tightened, and I tensed, letting out a hoarse groan as my cum shot down her throat. She drank me down as I continued to rub her clit, and seconds later, she came again. My hips shuddered as I shifted back and slowly pulled out of her mouth. Rubbing her throat gently, I crouched down to smooth her hair off her sweaty face.

"I knew I could do it," she said, her voice raspy while her eyes were alight with pride.

Spiderman style, I kissed her hard while she was still upside down. Her hands lifted to tangle in my hair, and when I pulled back, she made a sound of protest. "We still have a while before we need to be back at Sugar and Scotch."

Grinning, I moved to climb on the bed, pulling her to the head of it and tossing her against the pillows like she weighed nothing. She squeaked as I laid on top of her and kissed her again. Beaming against her lips I told her, "You're an insatiable little minx."

Her head tilted toward the ceiling as she laughed and drew her legs up to trap me between them. "I think you mean insatiable cougar."

CHAPTER TWELVE

THE PACKET OF PAPERS STILL FELT WARM, LIKE they'd just been printed, as I flipped through them. Every *t* looked crossed, every *i* dotted. No funny business. No loopholes. Just plain, simple, and straightforward.

Divorce papers.

Nothing more than what I was legally entitled to. Actually, it was much less, but that was for a reason. And perhaps one clause that made sure Scott couldn't come after Sugar and Scotch in any way once he'd signed his name. *If* he signed his name. But that was something I could worry about next weekend when I returned for the charity gala.

"Does everything look okay, Mrs. Tailor?" a soft voice asked behind me.

Sarah Lewis was a tough-as-nails divorce lawyer who specialized in cases like mine. I hadn't told anyone yet, not even Rylee, but I'd hired her months ago. I didn't want to confront Scott until I knew for certain he wouldn't be able to spin things his way and get a judge to turn things around on me.

Money talked, even if you thought you were the kind of person who couldn't be swayed by such a trivial thing. Trust me; you could be. And Scott had an endless supply and the means to get just about anyone to do his bidding.

But Sarah Lewis was discreet, and her team worked behind the scenes–after signing NDAs–until everything was in the perfect place to approach your cheating spouse successfully.

These last few months opened my eyes to the kind of life I wanted to live. New York no longer held any appeal for me. Jacksonville made me happy, and I felt like I had become the best version of myself while down there.

And Tyler, while not the reason I was finally doing this but definitely a bonus, had made me feel alive again. In a way I'd forgotten even existed. Don't get me wrong—I liked my life of luxury. But Ms. Lewis and her team had figured out a way for me to keep my condo and live the rest of my life comfortably.

I just had to give up everything else I was entitled to.

I'd have to give back the family ring, which I was completely fine with, and give up my half of everything we owned. New York didn't exactly *have* to recognize the infidelity clause in our prenup, it would depend on the judge, but that was part of the work the lawyer who now sat in front of me did.

And from the looks of it, she did her job well.

"I think this all looks great, Ms. Lewis. I'm just a little worried about whether they will adhere to the infidelity clause in the prenup. It's going to be harder to fight if they don't." I pushed the packet away and leaned back in my chair, setting my elbow on the arm and perching my chin in my hand.

She smiled and gave a small shrug. "I think Mr. Tailor will make this difficult, regardless of the court's decision. Even with all you're giving up, I don't think he will want to give *you* up."

A pregnant pause filled the small room, and her eyes flitted back and forth on the table between us as she looked like she was internally deciding how to ask her next question. "If you don't mind me asking, why now? Why not when your husband started stepping out on you publicly?"

I gave a short laugh before taking a sip of the coffee her secretary had brought in for me. It was not a dirty martini, as the occasion called for, but it would do until I could return to Jacksonville. "I'm sure you've heard it all before. Why leave the husband when you can take the money and do what you want with your life? They have their fun, and you have yours. Everyone wins."

"But that's not really a marriage, is it?" she asked, though it was more a statement than a question. I nodded in agreement.

"It's an *old money* way of life. But I'm not that woman anymore. I married into it, and I came from nothing. As much as I don't want to go back to having nothing, sometimes I think it's better than having *everything*." My gaze focused out the window behind her. The sun had started to set, casting an orange glow over the city that lit up the colors of fall. I loved New York this time of year, but not enough to keep coming back.

"So, what changed your mind?"

My eyes found hers as a small smile spread across my face. "After a long time of settling for *'that's just the way things work in this world,'* I remembered how to be *happy* again."

I'D SOMEHOW GOTTEN lucky enough to spend the week in New York finishing up things for the charity gala without Scott coming home. But five days without Tyler had left me feeling like a needy dog whose owner had gone on vacation. When I got home, all I wanted to do was drape across his lap while he rubbed my belly.

Well, much lower than my belly.

I'd almost said fuck it and bought him a ticket to New York, but Rylee had quickly reminded me that I liked his cock warm and hard, not soft and cold. Which is what he'd be if Scott had come home and caught another man in our bed.

So, I'd spent the last five days agonizingly alone with no orgasms in sight because, for his birthday, Tyler had asked me to refrain from touching myself while I was gone. He'd said he wanted to be the only one to make me come, not even if we were sexting or talking over the phone.

As I drove from my condo to Sugar and Scotch, I remembered what he'd told me the first night I was back in the city.

"Trust me, Wifey. There will be a day when I watch you come on your fingers to the sound of my voice before I lick up every last drop. But I want you wound so tight when you come home, that you beg me to fuck you the second you walk in the door."

A wave of arousal warmed between my legs, and I squeezed my thighs together as I sped up. God, he was so fucking hot. I had no fucking clue how I held off for so long when it came to him. But as much as I *did* want him to fuck me the second I walked into his house, I needed to hurry and finish helping Rylee set up the bar for the birthday party we were throwing him later tonight.

Halloween was two weeks away, so we were surprising him with a costume party. It was also why the board for the gala had decided to go with a masquerade theme for the charity event, so while I was picking up my mask for that, I'd also picked up costumes for Tyler and me for tonight. He had no clue what I had planned, but I'd called in the order a few days ago and put a rush on it, and I couldn't wait to see the excitement on his face when I showed him.

As I pulled into the back of the bar, my phone started to ring, and Tyler's name popped up on my dashboard screen. I didn't want him to know I was back yet, I'd taken an earlier flight than I'd told him, but the ridiculously needy part of me wanted to hear his voice.

"Hi, birthday boy," I sang while parking.

"Aww, thanks, Wifey. But it's not my birthday till tomorrow. You headed to the airport?"

"Yeah, I gotta run to my house first after I land, then I'll head to your place?"

"Sounds good. I just wanted to check in. I hadn't heard from you all day." He sounded worried, and his tone made me feel bad. He'd been anxious about the possibility of Scott showing up, and me going off-grid probably hadn't helped that.

"Sorry, I just got caught up with last-minute preparations for the gala. I'll see you soon, though."

"Alright. See you soon."

We hung up, and I bolted out of my car and into the building. "I'm late, I know. I'm sorry. My flight got stuck on the tarmac waiting to deboard, and for whatever reason, my cell wouldn't pick up service on the plane," I yelled out while rushing through the doors to the front of the bar.

Rylee and Riya both turned to look at me with huge smiles as I came to an abrupt stop and looked around in awe. "You guys, this looks amazing!"

The entire bar was covered in stretchy spider webs with fake spiders in different colors and sizes. Giant bats hung from the ceiling, along with candles that looked suspended in the air. Random skeletons sat at tables throughout the room. There was a giant pumpkin king figurine just inside the entrance, the eyes and mouth aglow with a flickering light that made the giant pumpkin head eerie as fuck. Smaller pumpkin baskets were hanging from its arms, filled with candies and small party favors for all the guests we'd invited.

The stools at the bar were covered in sheets that made them look like ghosts, and there were clear cauldrons along the bar top filled with various colored punches—some of them even had smoke overflowing from the top. Between the cauldrons were various dishes covered in plastic wrap, with foods that looked like human body parts. And liquor bottles stripped of their labels and replaced with ones that said things like *poison* and *dragon blood* written in chalk.

"Do you like it?" Rylee asked with glee, her bright pink lips turning up in a smile that looked like it hurt her cheeks.

"Rylee, this is amazing. You guys, I don't even know what to say. I should have been here to help, but there's no way you two did all of this by yourselves in the last hour." I looked at them both skeptically, with a smile, as they grinned at each other.

"Hell no, I made Chance get the guys to do it.

They started this morning. Riya and I just finished mixing drinks and making the food," Rylee explained.

They were both already dressed in their costumes. Riya was dressed like a sexy Cleopatra and even had rubber snakes coiled up her arms and neck. Rylee was dressed as a flapper girl, and I knew Chance had gotten a 20's-style suit with a fedora to match. Her engagement ring sparkled on her finger like a beacon of pink, and it warmed my heart that my best friend had finally found her forever.

"Guests are going to be arriving soon. We wanted the party to be in full swing when you guys got here," Riya stated excitedly.

"I figured you could just surprise Tyler by showing up at his place early. Maybe sneak in a little sexy time, since lord knows that boy is gonna blow just by looking at you." Rylee laughed.

One of their phones dinged on the bar top, and Riya reached over to grab it. Her cheeks turned red as she handed the phone over to Rylee. "You forgot to turn off previews again."

Rylee grinned at her phone and then smirked at Riya. "What can I say? Chance makes me feel like a dirty little slut, and I love every second of it." She typed a reply and shoved her phone down the front of her dress. "He's on his way here, so you get going to your blue-balled baby."

"You two are so much cooler than any other bosses I've had before." Riya laughed as she shook her head, the rubber snakes bouncing with her movement, making them look alive.

"Seriously, you two are the best. Thank you," I said, reaching out to hug them both.

"That's what friends are for," Rylee replied.

"Does this mean I'm part of the friend group now?" Riya asked.

Rylee and I looked at each other with large smiles before looking back at her and simultaneously exclaiming, "Absolutely."

THE DOOR to Tyler's house opened before I could even reach out to grab the handle. As soon as I stepped over the threshold, Tyler's arms wrapped around me from behind as he nuzzled my neck. "You had to have already been here when we talked, Wifey. Why all the secrecy?" he whispered in my ear.

Spinning around in his arms, I held mine out to the side since there were multiple garment bags in my hands. "You know how we said we were all gonna get together for your birthday tomorrow?"

He looked at me with a skeptical grin. "Yeah."

"Well, we are actually going to do it tonight. In costumes! Ta-da!" I sang while lifting the bags.

"The four of us are gonna hang out in costumes? This totally sounds like my thing, but I'm surprised it's something you'd do." He laughed, leaning in to kiss me lightly. "Still doesn't explain why you're being so secretive."

His hands wandered from my waist down to my ass, and he squeezed hard, pulling me to him. I yelped and jumped back slightly. "Uh-uh, Pup. We gotta get dressed and go."

"I haven't seen you for five days, and you want to leave instead of letting me fuck you senseless?" He stepped toward me, and I smirked, taking another step back.

"We might be going somewhere other than Chance and Rylee's." Spinning around, I headed down the hall to his bedroom. I laid two garment bags on his bed and took the other to the closet to hang up for the other surprise I had planned for him later.

"Wifey, are you throwing me a birthday party?" he singsonged, watching me from where he leaned against his doorframe.

Exiting his walk-in closet, I jerked my chin toward the bags on his bed. "Open them up."

Tyler looked like a kid at Christmas. His face lit up as he raced to the bed to unzip the bags. When he saw what was in them, he turned around, staring at me wide-eyed. "Are you for real?"

Laughing, I walked over to stand beside him and looked down at the garish amount of green and yellow that stared up at us. "I figured these were the perfect costumes for you and me. Even though yellow is *so* not my color. And I could never pull off red hair in real life."

Reaching down for the short copper-colored wig, I placed it on my head. "What do you think?"

"I think you'll look hot in this jumpsuit, even if it's yellow, Miss O'Neil." He reached down and grabbed the purple bandana from his bag and tied it around his head before he shouted, "Cowabunga, dude!"

Shaking my head, I leaned over to give him a brief kiss. "Next year, I've already decided we're going as Cruella and a dalmatian."

Tyler paused in taking the rest of his costume out of its bag. "Next year?"

My cheeks turned pink, the flush warming my skin as I turned and busied myself with taking out the rest of my outfit. "Yeah, you know. If I haven't taken you to the pound by then."

I felt him at my back before he whispered, "I'd like to take you to the pound right now, but not the kind you're thinking of."

"Tyler, stop it. We're going to be late." Laughing, I gently nudged him back with my shoulder. "Get dressed, Pup."

He laughed as well and started to remove his clothes. "Woof."

"OH MY GOD, you guys look so cute! Donatello and April O'Neil! How perfect!" Rylee cried out when she saw us.

Tyler looked around the bar in awe. "Holy shit, you guys did all of this for me?"

"Technically, the guys did the decorations while I distracted you earlier. But, dude, of course, we did this for you. Happy birthday, man," Chance said, stepping forward to give Tyler a man hug.

"Happy birthday, Ty!" Rylee sang out as she hugged him after her fiancé.

Tyler looked like he was struggling with his feelings, so I wrapped an arm around his waist and kissed his cheek. "Happy birthday, Pup." Then I slid my hand down and squeezed his ass.

He jolted and grinned at me. "This means a lot. Thank you, guys."

Chance threw an arm around Tyler's shoulders, and they left to grab a drink while Rylee and I watched them walk away. "Damn, we're lucky," she stated.

"Yes, we certainly are." I admired Tyler's physique in his green turtle costume and sighed wistfully.

Out of my peripheral, I could see her turn to look at me, and I tore my eyes away from Tyler's ass to return her gaze. She gave me a cheesy grin as she nudged my shoulder with hers. "I know that look. I think someone has fallen in love."

My head swiveled back to watch as our men took shots with their friends. Love. Did I love Tyler? Had it crept up without me realizing it? He was so much younger than me. Weren't we just having fun?

But the more I thought about it, the more I realized that Rylee was right. In all the years we'd been together, I didn't think Scott had ever made me feel the way I felt when I looked at Tyler. When he looked at me. I thought about our nights together and the mornings I'd wake up in his arms. How we'd fallen into a routine, even before we started sleeping together.

How he just *knew* me. Sometimes I even felt like he knew me better than I knew myself. He made me feel seen and cared for. He made me feel *loved*.

And it hit me like a freight train that I had indeed gone and fallen in love with him.

I let out the breath I'd been holding, and my head felt dizzy. "Don't say anything to Chance, please."

"Hey, Sadie, it's okay. Babe, why are you crying?" I felt her delicate fingers gently wipe under my eyes as she spun me around so my back was to the rest of the room.

Blinking up at the ceiling a few times, I waited until the stray tears subsided, then looked down at my best friend, who was staring up at me with concern etched across her pretty face. "I don't know why I'm crying, honestly. I think...I think you may be right, Ry. But I don't want to tell him until this mess with Scott is sorted. I have to take care of my shit first."

"Of course. And you know I'm always here if you need anything. I know I've been spending all my time with Chance, but maybe you and I need to have a little getaway for just us girls. We could go down to the Keys?"

I didn't realize how much I'd missed spending time with her until now. Reaching out, I pulled her to me, biting my lip to keep the pesky tears that kept wanting to fall at bay. "I'd like that, Ry. And thank you for all of this."

She beamed up at me when we pulled away from each other. "I just expect to be the maid of honor at your wedding."

We laughed, and I turned back around, catching Tyler's eye from across the room. There was a look of concern on his face, but I shook my head and smiled. "Did I tell you what else I brought back from New York for him?"

I flashed Rylee a knowing smile. She looked confused before her eyes grew wide, and she squealed. "Oh my God, is it what we were talking about? Tell me it's what we talked about!"

She squeaked as I nodded my head. "Holy shit, that boy will not know what to do with you when he sees what you have in store for him. I think he might die of happiness. Or shock."

"Well, I certainly hope he doesn't die. But I expect he'll be more than happy...and shocked."

A FEW HOURS later found us back at Tyler's house. The party had been fun, but we'd skirted around each other all night, playing a sensual game of sending heated glances across the room when no one was looking. My skin felt like it was on fire by the time I peeled off the yellow jumpsuit and tossed the red wig on the floor of Tyler's bathroom.

I'd told him to get out of his costume and wait for me in his bedroom while I *freshened up*. And as I stared at myself in the mirror, ensuring everything was in place, I was turning myself on with anticipation of what he'd do to me when he saw what I now wore.

Tyler had once hung a giant portrait of me from my younger modeling days when I had posed in nothing but pearls. They'd been fashioned together specifically for me for a photo shoot, then placed on a bust and secured behind glass to be displayed in Scott's office at his request. The only time they'd left our penthouse was when designers requested to see them so they could fashion something similar for a movie they were working on about burlesque dancers.

But I'd taken the outfit and delicately packed it in my carry-on so I could make one of Tyler's biggest fantasies come true.

I fluffed my hair once more, having curled it before I'd put on the wig for the party. Once I was positive I looked like a bonafide sex kitten, I took a deep breath before quietly opening the door.

Tyler was lounging on his bed. He'd changed into gray sweats and wasn't wearing a shirt as he flipped through something on his phone. Turning the light off in the bathroom, I gently cleared my throat and took a small step forward.

His head turned, eyes finding me slowly before his breath caught, and he went as still as death. Swallowing thickly, his cock hardened, the outline apparent against his pants. My body tightened with want as my pussy grew slick. The sensation of my arousal coating the string of pearls that were nestled along my center and pressed against my clit, sent shocks of pleasure to the base of my spine. My nipples hardened as Tyler licked his lips and slowly got out of the bed to stand, his cock peeking out the top of his sweats.

"Am I dreaming right now?" he asked, his voice low and gravelly.

I shook my head slowly, and he sucked in a harsh breath. "Happy birthday to you," I sang seductively, à la Marilyn Monroe, slowly stepping forward. "Happy birthday to you." Another step. "Happy birthday, dear Tyler." When I was right in front of him, I raised a hand to walk my fingers down his chest. "Happy birthday to you." Then I reached into his pants and wrapped my hand around his cock.

Tyler's eyes were filled with lust as he took me in, and for a few seconds, we were both silent as I slowly pumped my hand down his shaft. Then, like a rubber band that was pulled too tight, he snapped. He grabbed me by my hips, lifting me and spinning to throw me on the bed as he growled, "I'm going to fucking ruin you."

CHAPTER THIRTEEN

Tyler

IF HEAVEN TRULY EXISTED, I WAS CONVINCED IT was between Sadie's thighs. She smirked up at me as I pulled my pants down and kneeled on the bed between her legs. Grabbing her ankles, I bent her legs up so that her pussy was on full display while she arched her back. She was soaked, and her juices coated the pearls—something I'd envisioned as I'd jerked off a hundred times before, when her portrait hung above my bed.

Slowly, I leaned down and ran my tongue against the string, knowing that the feeling would drive her crazy. "I've fucking thought about this moment so many times. You, in this outfit, bared to me, at my mercy. All the things I would do to you if I ever got the chance."

"Tell me. Tell me what you want to do to me, Tyler," she moaned and writhed against the bed as I gingerly flicked the pearls resting on her clit with my tongue.

My hands ran up her legs slowly, making sure she kept them bent and spread, before settling on her pearl-covered breasts. "I'd rather show you, since my mouth is going to be busy worshiping the only higher power I want to pray to."

Reaching between the strings, I pulled her nipples until they stuck out against the shiny cream beads. She cursed loudly as I pinched them between the pearls; at the same time, my teeth clenched around her clit, my tongue rolling the pearls against it in my mouth.

After a few moments of biting at her, then soothing the hurt with my tongue, I abruptly let her go and moved back as she sucked in a harsh breath and made a noise of protest. Grabbing my dick with one hand, I swiped the fingers of the other up her center before rubbing her juices over the crown. "Spread your legs for me. I want to see every glorious inch of that pussy."

She did as she was told and watched as I stroked myself slowly. "I can do that for you," she offered.

Shaking my head, I leaned forward, positioning my cock at her entrance. I pushed in two inches, the feeling of the pearls acting as a barrier between us, creating an oddly pleasant feeling that I felt all the way in the tips of my toes. "I want to fuck you bare tonight."

Sadie whimpered with need as she nodded

enthusiastically. I eased back out slowly and ran my head along the pearls, smacking it against her clit before quickly pushing back in, going further than before. The strings that made up her outfit were pliant and moved easily inside her, and we both groaned at the intense feeling of the foreign objects.

Bowing my head to pull one of her nipples between my lips, I sucked it hard and thrust into her further until I was a little more than halfway. Her hands tangled in my hair as she pressed her chest into my mouth. "I want to feel all of you, Tyler," she whispered against the top of my head.

Feeling like I'd explode at any second, I pulled back again, letting go of her nipple with a wet pop and pulling out of her completely. We both breathed heavily as we stared at each other, and I was torn between wanting to ravage her and wanting to make love to her slowly.

Because that's exactly what I felt as I gazed down at her. And it scared the shit out of me.

With a roar, I reached down and, with both hands, swiftly snapped the strings that held the pearls together. She gasped as the small beads went flying everywhere, some rolling down her body while others shot across the room. They scattered across the sheets as I hauled her to the head of the bed and shoved her into the mountain of pillows we'd accumulated over the last two weeks. Her gaze was pure molten desire as I surged forward and seated myself fully inside her.

Her knees instantly shot up and pressed into my sides as she let out a cry, but I didn't let up. Pulling back, I slammed into her again until our hip bones scraped against each other, and she was crying out with unbridled pleasure, "Harder. Fuck me harder, Tyler."

Shifting to oblige her, I grunted and snapped my hips with so much force, my bed frame knocked against the wall with a resounding bang. Her hands pulled my face down to kiss me, our tongues fighting for dominance and our teeth scraping against each other like we were trying to devour the last meal we'd ever eat. Her nails scraped along my back, causing me to let out a hiss, sure that she drew blood after one arduous thrust.

My weight fell to my knees as I wrapped one hand beneath her lower back and pulled her up to me as I drove into her, and she bit my lip, sucking it into her mouth with the sudden change in position. I felt like I couldn't sink into her any deeper, like I was trying to fuse our souls together as our movements grew erratic and sweat poured from our bodies.

There was a faint hint of a coppery tang mixed with the unmistakable heavy weighted scent of sex, and I felt blissfully euphoric as her inner walls clenched around me. "I'm going to come," she cried out hoarsely.

Her nails broke my skin, and her legs tightened around me as my body spasmed. I spilled my release into her as she came at the same time. Our bodies were pressed together so tightly that I felt her walls flutter around me as my cock pulsed with every stream of cum I emptied into her. Our hips slowly continued to rock together as our eyes locked, and I leaned down to kiss her softly.

My cock was still half hard as she threw her head back, my lips following hers as I swallowed a quiet cry when she came again. The entire moment was transcendent as we gazed at one another, basking in the afterglow. I didn't move off her, staying nestled inside her warmth as we lay there in contented silence. Her fingers traced idle shapes against my skin, and fifteen minutes later, I grew hard again and started rocking into her slowly, rewarded with a pleasured moan.

It was the best birthday I'd ever had, and I imagined there would never be another to top it.

I also knew by the end of the night that I was royally fucked.

THINGS HAD CHANGED between Sadie and me the night of my birthday party. We both knew it, but we continued to avoid the truth as we spent the rest of the weekend, and the following week, wrapped so deep in each other, we didn't know where one of us ended and the other began.

Fucking Sadie was my favorite hobby. Making love to her was my greatest privilege.

She'd gone back to New York this morning for her gala. My gut had been twisted in knots since she left, making me feel sick.

"You okay, Ty? You've been super quiet all day," Chance observed as we were on our way to a client's house.

Shrugging, I looked out the passenger window of his truck. "Just irritated that Sadie is going to be with *him* this weekend."

He looked over at me with an empathetic smile. "You really like her, don't you? You guys seem different since your birthday. Did something happen?"

I pulled on the collar of my plain black tee and reached over to turn up the air conditioning. "Everything changed last weekend, Chance. And I don't know what to do about it."

"What do you mean?"

"A large part of me thought that maybe after I'd had her, she would have lost her appeal to me," I admitted. It was the first time I'd allowed myself to be honest about how I felt in the beginning, and I was ashamed to admit it out loud.

His head snapped to look at me, surprise written across his face before he turned his eyes back to the road. "Are you saying it was all just a game to you?"

It was there—the undercurrent of judgment in his tone that we'd sworn we'd never use with each other. But I imagined he *would* be pissed, since the four of us had become so close over the past seven months.

"No, it was never a game. But it was always clear she wasn't ready to leave her husband. At least, not ready to fight him for a divorce. I was content with being her dirty secret. I pushed for it. I coerced her into this arrangement at every turn, thinking it would be easy to watch her go back to him. Thinking that I would be fine watching her walk away for good, eventually."

The silence stretched between us, both of us reflecting on the words we wanted to say next. Chance ended up speaking first. "And now? It seems like that's not the case anymore."

I stayed silent for a moment before sighing and shaking my head, desperate to pull up a hood that wasn't there. To hide and bury my emotions in a cocoon of cotton.

But it wasn't there to shield me, and I knew my mind had been made up. It had been made up the second our lips had touched that night in the bar kitchen. I just hadn't wanted to accept or admit it fully.

Until now.

My tone was despondent as I asked, "Do you think you could take me to the airport tonight?"

"The airport? Why?" Realization dawned on his features just seconds after he asked the question.

"Because now...now I'm in love with her."

"Fuck."

Yeah, fuck.

TIME SEEMED TO MOVE IN SLOW MOTION AS I gripped the manila envelope tighter and walked down the hall of the penthouse to Scott's office. I could hear him on the phone, arguing with someone over the price of a company, agitated and likely already in a bad mood.

Tonight was the charity gala, and we were set to leave soon. My hair and makeup had already been done earlier in the evening by the stylists I'd hired, and I'd given Claudia the night off so that when I approached Scott, there would be no witnesses to the argument I was sure would happen.

However, I was currently rethinking that decision.

I'd paced my walk-in closet for nearly twenty minutes, trying to decide whether or not I should give him the divorce papers before we left for the gala or after we got home. Before seemed like the best choice because I knew he wouldn't miss the event, and we'd have to play nice for appearance's sake. Whereas if I confronted him *after* the party, he'd likely be drunk and more difficult to deal with.

Our home seemed to glow as I walked through it. The city lights were lit up against the shadowy backdrop of the night, and its sunless presence seeped through the giant floor-to-ceiling windows, causing the lighting inside to have a dim glimmer.

It reminded me of Sugar and Scotch, and for a moment, I ached for home and the easiness of Jacksonville. But that couldn't be a permanent fixture in my life. Not until I handed the papers in my hand over to Scott and he agreed to sign them.

"I don't care what you negotiated with them. I didn't sign off on that, so go back to Travers and tell him it's double what you agreed on or nothing at all. And he's lucky I'm even still considering the deal with the shit he tried to pull. I didn't even need my lawyer to catch the mistakes you put in here, either. If you screw it up again, you're fired," Scott bellowed over the phone as I pushed the door to his office open.

He swung around in his giant wingback chair and slammed the phone down as his eyes landed on me. His jaw visibly clenched as his eyes swept down my body, taking in my appearance. He stood, buttoning his tuxedo jacket as he slowly walked around his desk and toward me.

"I have half a mind to bend you over my desk

and fuck you senseless before we leave. But I'm wound too fucking tight and wouldn't last a minute buried in your golden cunt. And I would hate to leave my wife unsatisfied." His voice was husky as he slowly backed me against the wall.

I swallowed thickly as my body tightened against my will. The base of my spine tingled as he settled one hand on my waist and reached up to grab my chin with the other. Before he could lean in and kiss me, I slapped the envelope against his chest, and when he reached up to take it, maneuvered away from him.

"What is this?" he asked.

"Divorce papers," I responded softly, staring out the window. I saw his reflection look at me sharply with incredulity before his features morphed slowly to insulted as he chuckled and tossed the packet of papers onto his desk.

"Excuse me?"

Sighing, I turned to face him. "I think we both know this has been a long time coming, Scott. I'm not asking to keep anything that doesn't rightfully belong to me. I'm willing to give up my half of our assets. I want to keep my condo in Florida and alimony–at a much lower rate than it *should* be."

"You won't get shit because you're not fucking divorcing me, Sadie."

"We can do this the easy way or the hard way. It's no secret that you cheat, and there's bound to be a judge somewhere in this city that can't be bought. Surely you're not actually surprised?"

His chest rose and fell in a shallow rhythm, and the vein in his temple protruded as his skin flushed an angry vermillion. Our gazes remained locked, mine resolute while his grew wild with fury. "How long have you been planning this?" he spat.

"For a while. Once I found out you lied about the girls and the club. It doesn't have to be messy, Scott. We can do it quietly, and I can disappear," I said evenly.

He let out a feral cry as he swiped everything off the surface of his desk. Papers fluttered through the air as pens, paperweights, and his laptop fell to the ground with a deafening crash.

I was surprised at my ability to stay calm and rational as I watched my husband of twenty years lose his composure. You'd think I had just told him he'd lost all his money with the way he was acting.

"You think you're so clever, don't you? Going behind my back to put this together. Well, guess what, Sadie? All it takes is sending a P.I. to Jacksonville to see what has you preoccupied down there. Do you think I can't find something to use against you? You'll end up with nothing. I'll take your condo, and I'll take your little bar. Will that be worth it? Watching everything you've worked so hard for come crashing down around you? Will it be worth putting your friend through that? Watching her dreams get crushed all because you can't handle our way of life."

I bit the inside of my cheek, my heart rate spiking as he taunted me. A small part of me had hoped he would be civil and that we could end this amicably, but clearly, that wasn't going to happen. Leaving now would be a wise decision. Going to the gala without him and letting him cool off was the smart choice.

Instead, I shrugged, took a few slow steps toward him, and called his bluff. "There's nothing to find in Jacksonville except a bar full of happy patrons. I've already ensured you can't touch it *or* Rylee. So, do what you have to do, I guess. I'm leaving for The Plaza now. You can either arrive with me or on your own, but for appearance's sake, you should probably be in the limo in the next ten minutes."

Reaching up, I fixed his slightly crooked bow tie before running my hands down his jacket's lapels, smoothing them out. He seemed to relax under the familiar gesture, his eyes searching my own for some sign that I'd been joking the whole time.

My heart rate returned to normal as my ruby-painted lips turned up in a simulated smile. "Tonight, no one will have any idea just how ugly things are about to get between us. We will be the picture-perfect couple we've always been. And in a few weeks, when news breaks of our impending split, everyone will be amazed at how good of a show we put on for them."

I patted my hands against his chest and moved to leave his office. "Sign the papers, Scott. And be in the limo by the time I'm ready to go."

My heels clicked on the shiny surface of the floor as I walked away, not bothering to see his reaction to my words. But he yelled at my back, "I'm not signing them!"

Smirking, I grabbed my clutch and the mask that sat next to it on the small table in the foyer. "We'll see about that."

CHAPTER FIFTEEN

Tyler

Opulence dripped from every corner of the Grand Ballroom at The Plaza. The massive columns surrounding the room were draped in black gauze with glittering crystals that caught the dim glow of the chandeliers, making the entire ballroom glitter like the night sky. The large dance floor in the middle of the room was surrounded by tables with deep crimson tablecloths and large golden candelabra centerpieces with strings of pearls and dead roses trickling from them.

It was a sea of black with the occasional hint of red, gold, and silver. The men were all in their finest tuxedos, while the women wore extravagant gowns with lavish masks encrusted with jewels. There were several men who'd opted not to wear masks, much to their wives' dismay, it seemed.

Wanting to remain anonymous until the time was right, I'd picked up a simple black mask that covered the top part of my face. Its satiny material matched the lapels of the Tom Ford tuxedo I'd gotten earlier, but I didn't plan on wearing it all night. Just long enough to find Sadie and take her for a spin on the dance floor.

I'd arrived early, already in the shadows behind the columns, waiting to make my move when she and Scott finally showed up.

They walked into the ballroom, her arm looped through his and I was not prepared for the rush of fire that shot through my veins at seeing them together in person. Scott's smile was so tight that he looked in pain as he stared down at her.

Sadie, however, was radiant. Her smile was full and charming, and she shined brighter than anyone else in the room. Even if it was just for the paparazzi, they were putting on a show, and it calmed my nerves.

Her hair was down and curled around her bare shoulders, and her face was done up with heavy makeup as if she were about to do a photoshoot. She wore a strapless, black satin gown that hugged every curve. The top of the bodice curled into points on both sides with see-through material, creating a cat eye design that accentuated her exquisite breasts, while the skirt fell in heavy panels to the floor and trailed behind her. There was a slit so high on one side that her tanned thigh was entirely on display. Lace gloves extended up her arm, ending just above her elbows, and they shimmered as she moved, matching the delicate lace and sequined mask that rested on her face, and was secured with a simple black ribbon.

Every woman in the room watched her with envy, while the men looked at her with desire as Scott paraded her around like a prized mare at a show.

I watched them for a while as they mingled. He acted every part of the doting husband while she played the role of the trophy wife of the Upper East Side elite.

It made me sick. Even if I knew it was all an act.

They danced together, and when they weren't on the dance floor or mingling with guests, they talked to each other through clenched teeth and frozen smiles. Finally, something she said must have set him off as he stormed away from her under the guise of taking a call. And I decided it was time to make my move.

Sadie was turned toward the bar, ordering a drink as I came up behind her, leaning in to whisper, "Dance with me."

Startled, she spun around to face me, and her red-painted lips parted in astonishment. I didn't give her a chance to respond, gently grabbing her hands and pulling her with me to the dance floor.

"Tyler? What on Earth are you doing here?" she asked in anxious surprise as she looked around frantically, as if she were afraid Scott would see us. I genuinely didn't care if he did.

"Well, so much for masks concealing your identity. I missed you, Wifey. Besides, I couldn't stand the thought of him being the one who got to see you in this dress. I'm going to have fun peeling it off you later," I spoke quietly into her ear.

"Tyler!" she admonished as her eyes grew wide, and she looked around to make sure no one heard me. My lips turned up in a grin as I spun her away before pulling her back into my arms, closer than before. "How did you get a ticket? It's almost four thousand dollars a head."

My cheek brushed against her temple as I laughed. "And?"

She pulled her head back and glanced over my shoulder as my hand tightened on her waist. "Scott is looking," she warned, forgetting her previous question. And it was just as well, because this wasn't the time or place to explain how I'd been able to afford a ticket.

Though Sadie would know everything by the end of the night.

"Good. Let him watch while his wife falls for another man." Before she could respond, I turned and dipped her low, moving slowly as the tension between us grew. Her hand gripped my arm, the other wrapped in my hair as I lowered my face closer to hers. "God, you're fucking beautiful," I whispered before pulling her up.

A quick glance in Scott's direction showed him clenching his jaw hard enough that I could tell from our place on the dance floor. One hand was in his pocket, while the other gripped a glass of amber-colored liquid as he talked to a group of men, though his focus remained on us.

"He's already suspicious, Tyler. You're lucky he doesn't know who you are because you're actually wearing a mask, but he's probably going to have his men tail you for the rest of the night," Sadie said nervously.

She sounded concerned for me, and I frowned, leaning forward to put my lips close to her ear as I told her, "Don't worry about me, Wifey. And promise me you'll let me explain everything when I see you later."

Before she could ask me what I would need to explain, I let her go and disappeared through the crowd, leaving her on the dance floor. As the sea of masks and tuxedo jackets consumed me, I turned to see Scott taking my place—scowling as he drew Sadie's attention, preventing her from seeking me out.

BIDING MY TIME, I sipped on Macallan. Tonight wasn't just about telling Sadie I loved her. It was about ensuring she knew she'd be safe to leave her husband with me by her side. And in order to do that, I needed to let go of the hatred I held for Scott Tailor.

A hatred that was etched deep in my soul and was due to a lot more than just the way he treated her.

A familiar face appeared at the bar a few guests down from me, and I realized this was my opening. Reaching up to pull the mask off my face, I left it on the bar and walked over to a man I'd known since childhood.

Weylan Kennedy and his wife, Margo, had been friends with my parents for years. His son, Tripp, was a few years older than me, and we'd spent a few summers in the Hamptons playing together and getting into trouble when we were younger.

After my parents died in a car crash when I was ten, they tried to keep in touch, but Ashlee and I had gone to live with our grandmother in Illinois, and eventually lost contact. I'd seen them a few times over the years, but their lifestyle wasn't something I'd wished to immerse myself in, and I think Weylan had given up the hope that I'd follow in my father's footsteps and become a successful businessman.

Success looked very different to me, than it did to them. The way I saw it, I *had* become a successful businessman. But as soon as Sadie had entered my life, and I realized who she was, a small part of me wondered what would have happened had I returned to New York and asked Weylan to take me under his wing, like he had his son.

What type of revenge would I have sought? Would it have included Sadie?

And I wondered if she would hate me after she found out the truth.

The thought caused my steps to falter, making me pause to wonder if I was doing the right thing. Before I could make the decision, though, Weylan turned and caught sight of me. "Tyler? Is that you?"

Smiling, I reached out to shake the hand he offered. "I thought that was you, Mr. Kennedy. It's been a long time."

He laughed and pulled me into him for a hug. He was a few inches shorter than me, and I could tell his light brown hair was starting to gray, as his familiar scent of cigars and peppermint filled my nose. "Oh, my boy, call me Weylan! It's so good to see you! Have you seen Margo or Tripp? They're around here somewhere, you'll have to say hello, or Margo will never let me hear the end of it. How are things? How's Ashlee?"

He led me away from the bar as he spoke, so that we could let the other guests behind us get their drinks. "Things are good. Business is great, and Ashlee is still in Chicago, having the time of her life. Her boss is good to her, and she's really happy."

"That's so good to hear. You know, Margo was devastated when you didn't keep in touch. She'll be happy to see you. What are you doing *here*, by the way? Have you moved back to the city?" he asked as his attention was caught by something over my shoulder.

As I responded, he waved someone over. "No,

I'm not back in the city. As a matter of fact, I came here tonight to talk to–"

"Scott, come here. I want you to meet someone," he cut me off.

My whole body tensed, kicking into defense mode, as Weylan reached out and gripped the shoulder of the man I loathed. He smiled at me and stuck his hand out as Weylan introduced us. "Scott Tailor, this is Tyler Michaelson. Tyler, this is Scott and his beautiful wife, Sadie."

My heart dropped into my stomach as she came to stand beside Scott and looked at me like a deer caught in headlights. I silently prayed to whatever God was listening to make her forgive my actions in the next few minutes, because this interaction was not turning out how I'd imagined it would. But this was my chance to show her I was serious about us.

And I was going to take it.

"Yeah, we know each other. Nice to see you again, Sadie." Confusion found its way onto Scott's face while Sadie stared at me like a beautiful living statue, frozen in terror.

"How do you two know each other?" Scott asked. I could see the wheels turning in his head while he stared at her, waiting for an explanation.

A red flush crept up Sadie's neck, and I wished I could tell her to breathe. That she had nothing to worry about anymore. This was my grand gesture. I would let go of my anger toward Scott, but I wouldn't let *her* go.

He looked back at me, his brow furrowed in suspicion, as Sadie finally took a breath and cleared her throat. Her voice was barely more than a whisper as she said, "Tyler also lives in Jacksonville."

Scott's head whipped to the side as he scrutinized her, and I watched as he pieced something together in his mind. He observed Sadie as she watched me, uncertainty painted on her face behind her mask.

"That's right. You did settle in Florida, didn't you? How do you like it down there? I like the sun, don't get me wrong, but I couldn't handle the hurricanes," Weylan cut in, completely oblivious to what was happening right in front of his eyes.

"How do *you* know each other?" Sadie asked, motioning with a flute of champagne between Weylan and me before she drained her glass.

Scott's gaze cut back to me as Weylan explained, "I was good friends with Tyler's dad when he was younger. They lived here in the city until the car crash. Tragic accident. Scott, I think you were trying to buy Thomas' company at the time, weren't you?"

A look of plain horror crossed Sadie's face as she glanced between her husband and me. I schooled my features to remain passive while Scott replied, "We were in the middle of making a deal, yes. I wasn't aware you were his son."

My chest hurt from the lack of air my lungs were getting since I had stopped breathing when he'd started to answer. Sadie looked like she was about to cry, and if she gripped her champagne flute any tighter, I feared it would shatter in her hand.

"If you'll excuse me for a moment, I see someone I need to talk to. Tyler, don't leave without coming to see me again. Margo will skin me alive if you don't say hello. Scott, Sadie, always a pleasure. Great party, Sadie, as always," Weylan said, before disappearing through the crowd.

Scott watched him go before his eyes found mine again. A carefully constructed and fake empathetic smile on his face as he said, "I was sorry to hear about what happened to your parents. They were good people."

"They *were* good people. It's a shame someone had them killed," I fired back instantly. The secret I'd been carrying around for so long, the suspicion I had about Scott being the reason my parents were dead; it was all out in the open now.

The meaning behind my words wasn't lost on him as he drew himself to full height and raised an eyebrow. "You think someone had them killed? Now why would you think that?"

Sadie let out a breath, and my face eased as my attention turned to her. "Sadie, maybe you should go grab another drink."

"You seem awfully familiar with my wife. Care to explain why?" Scott snapped as he stepped forward, angling himself in front of her as if he needed to protect her from me.

"Tyler owns the landscaping business that takes

care of Sugar and Scotch." Her voice was stronger as she seemed to recover from the shock. "He's friends with Chance. That's all."

She smiled at me—a fake, plastic grin, as she stepped closer to him. The simple smile curled into a beam as he looked down at her while she reached out to touch his arm. "I am parched. I think I will grab another glass of champagne. Come find me soon. Tyler, good to see you again."

I felt it like a physical blow in my gut as she walked away dismissively, even though I knew it was all a show. I had taken it a step too far and should have told her everything before confronting Scott.

That was my mistake.

Scott's attention turned back to me, and I clenched my jaw in preparation for his inevitable *stay away from my wife* speech. "You know, I actually liked your father. He was a good businessman. He knew when to take risks, but he always struggled with knowing when to give up and admit defeat."

Fury shot through me, and his words took me by surprise. He was the reason my parents were dead, and his suggestive comment was as good as an admission to me. My fists clenched in tandem with my jaw as disgust poured from me, and he picked up on it, smirking as he looked me up and down.

Putting his hands in his pockets, he took a few steps forward so that he could speak in a low tone that was only meant for my ears. "If I remember correctly, you have a younger sister, isn't that right?

Be careful, Tyler. Don't make the same mistake your father did."

My fists clenched at my side, and I almost hit him. *Almost.* But that was exactly what he expected me to do, and I wouldn't give him the satisfaction. Grinding my teeth together so hard I thought they might crack, I stared straight ahead as he took a step back and delivered a low laugh.

"You should take your landscaping business somewhere else, far away from Sadie's bar, if you know what's good for you. Now, if you'll excuse me, I'm going to go kiss my beautiful wife." He smirked in victory and turned to find Sadie.

The words were out of my mouth before I could stop them. "Let me know how my dick tastes."

He pivoted abruptly, and his gaze snapped to mine, murder evident in his eyes. Before he could say anything, I turned and disappeared through the crowd, searching for somewhere to wait until I could get Sadie alone again.

CHAPTER SIXTEEN

MY STOMACH CHURNED VIOLENTLY.

Reaching up to untie the ribbon that held my mask in place, I made my way through the crowd, heading for the bathroom. My first instinct was to call Rylee, but I felt like I could barely breathe, let alone talk.

The information that had just been thrown in my face swirled in my mind as I replayed every single interaction Tyler and I had ever had.

He'd had to have known who I was the first day we met. But had he known before or after? I guessed he'd found out after our initial meeting, but before he and Chance returned to the bar that night. His comments about Scott– they were odd, but he'd done such a great job at covering them up in mock concern for me having a cheating husband.

Barking out a laugh, I drew the attention of random guests as I passed them. It had all been a lie.

Every moment, every kiss, every touch. All to get back at Scott because Tyler thought he killed his parents.

The door to the bathroom swung in easier than I had anticipated, and it banged against the wall. A few women who were crowded around the full-length mirror jumped as the noise echoed, and I smiled apologetically before moving to the sitting area to take a seat on a plush, blush-colored velvet chair.

Attempting to get my racing heart under control, I took deep breaths in through my nose and out through my mouth. My chest hurt, and tears stung my eyes, but I stubbornly refused to let them fall because I wasn't about to ruin my makeup.

My clutch vibrated in my lap, and I pulled my phone out to see that Tyler had just sent me a message.

> Meet me in the foyer. Please, Sadie. Let me explain.

Sighing, I tossed my phone back into my clutch without responding. Did I *want* to let Tyler explain? I wasn't entirely sure. Part of me honestly wanted to confront Scott and ask whether or not he had anything to do with Tyler's parents' car crash.

Scott may not have been the greatest husband, but I couldn't see him putting a hit on anyone or, God forbid, murdering someone himself.

And Tyler's parents died when he was ten, meaning Scott and I had been married at the time.

Which reminded me that I was already a married adult when Tyler was just a child.

I scoured my memories for a time when I could have possibly met his parents, but couldn't remember a single time when Scott introduced me to a Thomas Michaelson.

By the time I left the bathroom, I wasn't sure how much time had passed since I'd gone in. The crowd wasn't as large, and it didn't take me long to find Scott sipping brandy as he talked to Mick Charles, one of the Senators of New York.

Glaring at the tall, dark-haired man as I sidled up to them, I reached out to touch Scott's elbow. "I'm not feeling well. I think I'm going to head home."

"Sadie, you look lovely as ever. How are you this evening? Kate was sorry she couldn't make it. She misses you, though. You two should get together soon," Mick suggested with a smug grin on his face.

Scott peered down at my hand where I still touched him, before slowly dragging his gaze to meet my eyes. "Sadie hasn't been around much. She's been spending all her time down in Jacksonville."

He removed his hand from his pocket and curled it around my waist, pulling me into him as Mick replied. "Florida? Why on Earth would you want to spend your time there?"

Rolling my eyes, I answered, "I happen to like the beach."

"Amongst other things," Scott said under his breath. Louder, he told me, "I'll have Eddie pull the limo around. I still have matters to attend to here, so I'll see you at home later."

His head dipped to kiss me, and I almost flinched back, but his grip on my waist tightened in warning and reminded me we were still putting on a show. So, I relented and met his kiss with a thorough look of adoration, and his grip relaxed as Mick chuckled.

Stepping back, I glared at Mick once more. "Tell your *wife* I said hello, and I'm sorry she couldn't make it. Scott, I'll see you at home."

"Yes," his voice was direct and matter of fact, "you certainly will."

I didn't put any thought into his tone as I walked away, moving between the remaining guests and the columns that lined the room with hurried steps. I wondered if Tyler was still waiting for me in the foyer or if he had left. Glancing around as I passed through the large lobby, I didn't see him anywhere. My shoulders sagged in disappointment, and I went outside to wait for the limo while checking my phone to see if he'd messaged me again, only to find that the battery had died.

"Shit," I cursed as our limo approached the curb. Our driver, Eddie, opened the door for me, and I thanked him with a small smile before getting in and moving to the driver's side of the wide backseat. Moments after he shut the door behind me, it opened again, and I let out a startled yelp as Tyler got in quickly and paused to make sure he shut the door at the same time Eddie shut his as he climbed in behind the wheel.

"What are you doing?" I hissed.

He motioned for me to be quiet and raise the partition that separated the back of the limo from the front. I did, and to his credit, Eddie didn't say anything as his eyes flicked to the rearview mirror and caught mine before glancing at Tyler and then back at the road.

Once the partition was up, I turned to see Tyler looking at me with a pained expression. "Sadie, I'm so sorry that happened the way it did."

He reached for me, and I jerked away from his touch. "So it was all a lie, then? You did it to get back at Scott because you think he killed your parents? Scott may be many things, Tyler, but he's not a killer."

Tyler's eyes hardened and narrowed. "I don't think you have any idea what kind of person your husband is, Sadie. But that doesn't matter right now. What matters is that you know *none* of it was a lie. Yes, by the time Chance and I showed back up at Sugar and Scotch, I did know who you were. But it didn't matter to me, because from the *second* I laid eyes on you, I wanted to make you mine. I had given up on the thought of revenge long before we met, I swear it. I never wanted to get involved in your world here, and I never even knew about you until I met you. Yes, I knew Scott was married, but I had no clue to who, and I didn't keep tabs on him. Please believe me."

"How do you expect me to believe that?! You tried *so* hard to get me to give in to you. And now I feel like *all* of it was a show! I feel like you pushed so hard because you just wanted to hand a giant *'fuck you'* to Scott."

"Sadie, I swear it's the truth. Trust me. It was a complete shock to find out you were married to him. But getting with you wasn't meant to be a *fuck you* to Scott." He placed his hands on either side of my face, then scooted closer to rest his forehead on mine, my eyes closing with the intimate gesture.

"Sadie, I love you."

My breath hitched as my eyes widened at his declaration, but before I could respond, he whispered, "You don't have to say anything back. Not until you're ready. But *please*, Sadie, please believe me. You *know* me. You know *us*. Nothing in these last seven months has been a lie."

A lone tear rolled down my cheek as I pulled my head back. He wiped it lightly with his thumb as his other hand traveled down to my hip.

"Come here," he said gently, pulling me into his lap.

He positioned me so that I was sitting on the seat between his spread legs, facing away as he drew me back against his chest. One arm wrapped under my breasts, as his other hand trailed down the front of my body to where the slit in my dress exposed my entire leg.

"Nothing I ever said to you was a lie," he whispered as his hand slipped between my bare skin and the front of my dress. My hips twitched on their own as he gently ran his fingers over the black satin of my underwear, right over my center. Reaching behind me, I threaded a hand in his hair while the other gripped his thigh.

"None of my touches were for anything other than to make you feel good." My underwear was already wet, but his gravelly voice, paired with his touch, was enough to make me come undone. He reached up with his other hand to cup my right breast as he kissed my neck gently.

"And yes, you may carry his last name. But it's *my* bed you're sleeping in. *My* name you're crying out in pleasure–" his fingers slid under the satin band, and he plunged two of them into me, "–and *my* cock you're coming on every night."

Biting my lip, I moaned as his fingers moved faster, and he added a third. His thumb found my clit while his other hand reached down my dress to pinch my nipple. His mouth wet against my neck as he latched on and suckled gently at the spot just under my ear.

He knew that drove me wild.

Sharp tingles ran through my body as my hips undulated against his fingers, chasing my orgasm. His cock was solid under my ass, pressing between my cheeks as I ground down against him, causing him to bite my skin as he groaned. "Come for me, baby."

His words ripped my release from me like a tidal wave, my cum coating his fingers as my knuckles flew between my teeth as I tried not to cry out too loudly. "Good girl," he praised, his voice husky as his fingers slowed inside me.

Lifting my foot, I pushed my heel against the seat on the side of the limo, using it for leverage as I pushed my ass harder into his cock. My hands pushed against the ceiling and roof while I continued rolling my hips to meet his, his sighs of pleasure in my ears. "Fuck, Sadie. You're gonna make me come."

"Mmhmm, that's the point," I moaned in a hoarse rasp and continued rocking my ass. He hugged me to him, and I felt his hips stutter. Then he swore and rested his forehead against my back as he came.

A few seconds later, he leaned back, pulling me with him as he removed his fingers from me and brought them to my lips. Drawing his fingers into my mouth, I licked them clean of my essence before he clutched my jaw, turning my head to crush his lips to mine. His tongue swept my mouth as he tasted me, and I turned in his lap to face him fully.

"Mrs. Tailor, we've arrived," Eddie's voice cut through the intercom.

I pulled back, wiping my mouth and fixing my dress while moving off Tyler. We spent a few minutes catching our breath as we stared at each other from across the seat we both were leaned back on. "Are you flying back tonight?"

He checked what looked like a vintage Rolex on his wrist and nodded. "My flight leaves in a few hours."

"I'll have Eddie take you to the airport. I fly back tomorrow, late afternoon. I'll see you then?"

"I don't like the idea of you being alone with him tonight," he said, tone full of worry.

"Yeah, I suppose I will have to do damage control." I thought about how angry Scott was before we left for the gala and whether I should tell Tyler I served him divorce papers. But I had a feeling Scott would drag it out as long as he could, and I didn't want Tyler involved in the mess it would inevitably become.

"I'll be fine, don't worry." Reaching over, I pressed the button for the intercom. "Eddie, can you take my friend to JFK, please?"

"Sure thing, Mrs. Tailor."

Tyler frowned before leaning over to kiss me softly. "I'll see you tomorrow?"

My hand cupped his cheek. "Of course. We can talk more then."

"Okay." He smiled at me, and I realized there was no way this man in front of me could have ever used me as a means of revenge. I *knew* I meant more to him than that. I *felt* it in his actions.

My hand dropped as I moved to get out of the

limo, and only after closing the door and watching it drive away did I realize I never told him I loved him, too.

A FEW HOURS, at most, were all I had before Scott came home. My steps were quick down the hall toward my bedroom to start packing more of my things before having to deal with the aftermath of tonight.

As I passed the living room, a light clicked on, making me jump and let out a sharp scream. Scott was sitting in a chair in the corner of the room, balancing a glass of amber-colored liquid on his knee with the tips of his fingers.

"Jesus Christ, Scott, you scared me," I uttered breathlessly, putting a hand on my chest. "I thought you had business to deal with? And how did you make it back before I did?"

He ignored my questions, staring at me solemnly for so long that I shifted uncomfortably. I wondered if he'd seen Tyler get in the limo at The Plaza. And I wondered what they'd said to each other once I'd left them alone at the party.

Surely Tyler wouldn't have...

"I gotta hand it to you, Sadie. I didn't think you had it in you." Scott chuckled as he rose from the chair. My blood froze in my veins as he stalked toward me slowly, and as my back hit the wall, I hadn't even realized I'd been retreating from him.

"What? Finally getting the nerve to divorce you?" My voice wasn't firm; instead, it came out soft and quiet.

"Don't play stupid with me. I knew there was a reason you started staying in Jacksonville longer. How long have you been fucking the kid?" He stopped a few feet away, and I could see the vein in his forehead bulging as his skin reddened.

Swallowing the lump in my throat, I replied, "I have no clue what you're talking about, Scott. Tyler and I are friends, nothing more."

The words had barely left my mouth before he hurled his glass at the wall next to me with a deafening shout. The sound of it shattering mixed with my surprised cry, as the stench of brandy filled my nose. Suddenly, he was there, crowding me as he grabbed my jaw and squeezed.

His grip was punishing. I pressed back into the wall to try and get further away from him, but he pinned me with his weight as he squeezed harder, causing me to whimper in pain. My hands tried to pull his arm away, but he wouldn't budge. He looked at me with wild eyes, nostrils flaring as he breathed heavily into my face.

"Don't you dare fucking lie to me. He as good as told me you fucking slept with him. Is that why you want a divorce? Is that why he was at the gala? You wanted to parade him in front of me because you knew I couldn't do a damn thing about it? Well, I have news for you, Sadie. End it. Now. Or I will fucking *kill* him."

Tears lined my eyes, and Scott pushed off me as he let go of my jaw. It felt locked, and I knew there would likely be bruising. My hand cradled it while moving it back and forth, trying to eliminate the stiffness.

"Did you have anything to do with his parents' crash?" I had to ask. Tyler had been right. Apparently, I didn't know Scott as well as I thought I did. Because the husband I knew would have never dared put his hands on me.

He laughed and shook his head as he turned to pour himself another drink. "No, I'm not that fucking stupid. Why do you think Simon killed himself? *He* was the one who ordered the hit, and the guilt ate at him until he couldn't take it anymore. Although, now I wish the damn kids had been in the car, too."

Letting out a cry, I slid down the wall. Simon had been Scott's brother. He'd never been cruel or struck me as the type to take his own life, leaving his child—Jackson—behind. The suicide had been devastating and confusing. And I wondered if Scott was just spinning more lies, because I couldn't see any truth in his revelation.

And his comment about Tyler and Ashlee being in the car—what kind of monster had I married?

"How can you say that, Scott?" I looked at him in horror.

His laugh sounded maniacal as he tipped his head back and drained a new glass of brandy, before spinning to face me. "Trust me, the thought of that fucking prick with his hands on you has me thinking far worse things than that."

Rushing across the room, he hauled me to my feet. My hair fell behind my shoulder at the harsh movement, and his eyes snapped to the place on my neck where Tyler had bitten me. Scott's breathing grew harsher, and his fingers tightened on my arms. "Did you think of him while you fucked me? You deceitful whore!"

Those words lit a fire in me, and I shoved him, putting all my weight into it so that he was forced to take a step back. "How dare you! How fucking *dare* you call me a whore! You parade women around all over the country, and you have the audacity to get pissed when I fuck someone else?!"

I didn't even care that I'd just admitted to sleeping with Tyler. Something in me snapped as I drew myself up and stepped toward him. The look of fury on his face faltered as mine morphed into pure rage.

"You want to know why I'm divorcing you, Scott? It's because I'm *tired!* I tried, for so fucking long, to make this work. But you never once tried for me. You just kept throwing money at me like I was a problem you could buy your way out of. But I am

YOUR WIFE! And maybe it was my fault for being complaisant for so long, but I can't do this anymore! I can't spend the rest of my life waiting for you to come home after you've been in bed with another woman, expecting me just to be fine with it. And I can't–I *won't*–spend the rest of my life being put second, when I deserve to be put first.

"Tyler makes me feel like I am his whole world, and he makes me happy. He makes me so happy that all the money in the world can't compare. So I *am* leaving you. And you can have the penthouse, the vacation homes, the cars, and the jewels. I only want him, and he wants me, too. And *that* is enough for me," I growled harshly.

"Like hell, you're leaving me to be with him," he spat back, pausing to run a hand through his disheveled hair. He cracked his neck as he straightened his tuxedo jacket. "Don't test me, Sadie. Do you want his and his sister's death on *your* hands? Because they will be. Call my bluff if you want. But if you go through with this divorce, if you continue seeing him, have fun sleeping at night after you bury him in the ground."

I let out a shaky breath, my resolve crumbling. If tonight had taught me anything, it was that I shouldn't underestimate my husband.

I'd never be able to live with myself if something happened to Tyler or Ashlee.

Was I willing to take that risk?

Should I talk to Tyler about this confrontation?

My chest ached, and tears started to descend on my cheeks once more.

"You will return to Jacksonville and take care of your affairs with Rylee at the bar. Hell, sweetheart, I don't even mind if you want to keep your condo and stay for a few days at a time to visit her. But you will *not* see Tyler Michaelson again, and trust me, I will know if you do." He stepped toward me again, and I flinched. The motion caused him to pause as he stared at me while I cried silently. After a few moments, he reached out to cup the back of my neck and gently kissed my forehead.

The broken glass crunched under his feet as he walked away to go to his office. I wasn't sure how long I stood in the middle of the mess he'd made. The smell of brandy permeated the air, and I poured myself a glass before pounding it back, the smooth sweetness warming my insides as it slid down my throat.

Hours later, when the sun started to rise and fill the penthouse with its yolky shafts of light, the sounds of Claudia sweeping up the glass reverberated in the otherwise quietness of my home.

As I poured myself a cup of coffee, Scott appeared at the kitchen entrance, freshly showered and in a pressed suit. Our eyes locked as he threw the manila envelope that contained our divorce papers in the trash.

Where they remained as I left for the airport later that day.

CHAPTER SEVENTEEN

Tyler

MY MOUTH TASTED LIKE I'D EATEN A RAW, bloody steak as my eyes cracked open. I groaned, instantly regretting it as a sharp stabbing sensation struck my chest.

My entire body hurt.

As I shifted to try and sit up, my chest seized and caused a coughing fit. Wheezy harsh breaths left my body, and my hands were covered in blood splatters when the coughs finally subsided.

What the fuck had happened last night?

Looking around, I realized I was on my couch, back in Jacksonville. My head fell against the back of it as I closed my eyes, trying to remember the events of the night before. How the fuck had I gotten here?

As the limo door shut, I watched Sadie walk into her building, throwing one last smile over her shoulder. Even though I knew she couldn't see through the tinted window, I grinned back letting out a satisfied sigh as we pulled away from the curb.

I was thankful she believed me. That she believed in us. But I was worried about what Scott would say to her when he got home later. I shouldn't have baited him. I shouldn't have shown up at the gala and blind-sided her, either.

We drove a few blocks before I realized we weren't heading toward the airport. Normally, I would have just assumed that Eddie knew where he was going and that perhaps he was taking a shortcut.

Except we were headed in the complete opposite direction.

The busy city lights grew dimmer, and the number of people on the sidewalks started to dwindle. Frowning, I hit the intercom button. "Excuse me? I think we're going the wrong way."

The static in response was ominous, and I pressed the button to lower the partition, but it wouldn't budge. As we turned into a dark alleyway, I reached into my pocket for my phone to try to message Sadie.

Before I could unlock the screen, the limo came to a halt, and the door to my left opened abruptly. "What the hell-"

Two pairs of arms as thick as my head roughly pulled me out of the vehicle. My fight-or-flight instincts kicked in, causing me to struggle. Swinging at the guy on my left, my fists connected with the side of his head, and he swore as pain exploded in my hand from being in the wrong position to properly throw a punch.

There was a faint ringing in my ears as everything seemed to happen in slow motion. A third man stepped forward and landed his fist on my stomach. The breath flew out of me, and my body buckled, but the two men holding my arms hauled me back up so the third could hit me repeatedly.

It was a setup. Eddie knew where to take me. These men had been waiting for me.

Trying to catch my breath, I coughed, and the man laughed as he swung at my face. My head whipped to the side, the loud crunch of my nose breaking against a fist reverberating in my skull, as the other guys dropped me. Warmth dripped from my nose and a salty, copper taste painted my lips. Rolling to my side with a groan, my body coiled into the fetal position as one of the men kicked me in the stomach, and another foot connected with my lower back.

The onslaught of pain continued, to the point where I thought I would black out at any moment. And just when I didn't think I could take anymore, there was a reprieve from the meaty fists and sharp-toed Oxfords.

My vision was blurry through my swollen eyes. Every shallow breath made my chest ache, and I was worried a rib might be broken. Everything was foggy, like my mind couldn't make sense of anything through the haze of agony.

"Open the door," a gruff, throaty voice said. It

sounded close to me, and I slowly turned my head in the direction it came from. The gravel on the pavement underneath me cut into my skin, but I barely registered the sharp pang as it dug into the side of my face.

A dark figure crouched next to me and patted my upturned cheek a few times. "Sorry, kid. But you fucked with the wrong man. The boss ain't happy with you. Says to watch your back or your sister will be next. Roughing up a female ain't my thing, but my colleagues over there? They like 'em young and tight if you catch my drift. So, whatever you did, I suggest you don't do it again."

"Fuck you," I managed to spit around a mouthful of blood. Outrage at the mention of them harming my sister rushed through my body.

An amused laugh filled my ears, accompanied by the sounds of feet walking closer. Someone rolled me roughly onto my back. "Lights out, kid."

There was an explosion of pain. Then everything went black.

That motherfucker.

They hadn't used his name, but I knew Scott had been the one who set the whole thing up. Instantly, I worried he may have done something to Sadie, too. But a quick sweep of my pockets informed me my phone was missing.

I struggled to stand, but breathing became a little easier as my body stretched out. There was no doubt my nose was broken, and I shrugged out of my tuxedo jacket and slowly walked to my bathroom. My reflection was a mess of purple and red. Blood covered the lower half of my face, and I opened my mouth to inspect my teeth, ensuring I still had them all.

I had no intention of dragging my ass to the hospital. Instead, I turned on my shower and let the steam fill my bathroom as I peeled off my dress shirt and pants. The water scalded my skin when I stepped under the spray and watched it turn red on the shower floor. My limbs felt heavy, and my movements were sluggish in my attempt to wash the blood.

After I finished, the face that stared back at me in the mirror looked like it had just gotten a nose job. Both eyes were bruised, and my nose was swollen but, thankfully, still intact and didn't look like it would need to be reset. My lower lip was split. Bruises littered my ribs, and though it hurt to breathe, I didn't think they'd been broken.

All in all, I felt like Scott's men could have done much worse. But I recognized the beating for what it was...a warning.

And I knew next time I might not be so lucky.

HOURS LATER, a soft knock pulled me out of my thoughts.

I'd searched for my phone everywhere earlier but

couldn't find it, and it had been stressing me out not being able to hear from Sadie. I hoped it was her—I didn't think I could handle any more surprises today—as I pulled the bag of ice away from my nose and got up, trudging over to answer the door.

As I opened it, Sadie's bright green eyes widened in surprise. "Tyler, what the fuck happened to you?"

Slumping against the door in relief to see that she was unharmed, I joked, "Got in a little scuffle with Eddie."

She looked beautiful, as always, in a pair of white denim shorts with a light blue button-up. Her hand lifted, starting to reach out like she would embrace me before she stopped and swallowed, tucking her hair behind her ear nervously instead. The sparkle of her wedding ring caught my eye with the motion, jarring me—she hadn't worn her ring in Jacksonville in months.

"Can I come in?" she asked with a hard edge to her voice.

"You could have just walked in. What's going on?" There was something off about how she acted, which put me on alert.

As soon as I closed the door, I turned, intending to pull her into my arms. She stepped out of reach and looked down at the floor, clutching her purse in front of her like a lifeline. "We need to talk."

The words were ones I'd hoped I would never hear from her lips. They never brought any good news. I'd heard them a million times before, right before someone was about to tell you how much you'd disappointed them.

"Did something happen when Scott got home last night?"

Her eyes traveled up my body, taking in my bruises. She winced as if in pain, before schooling her features as our gazes finally locked. "What did you say to him?"

The question took me by surprise. My words to him from the night before echoed in my mind as I stared at her stony face.

Let me know how my dick tastes.

"Sadie, I'm sorry. I shouldn't have said anything—"

"You're absolutely right. You shouldn't have." Her tone was icy. She'd never spoken to me like that, even when we'd first met.

I suddenly felt like a child about to be reprimanded by an adult. The melting ice pack in my hand was as cold as her voice, and I started to turn toward the kitchen to put it back in the freezer. "Yeah, well, it looks like I paid for it, doesn't it?"

Her hand found her hip as she scoffed, "Maybe you deserved it."

"What the actual fuck, Sadie? Are you serious?" Anger coursed through my veins at her words, and the adrenaline momentarily masked the pain as I spun back around to face her fully.

"What did you think would happen if you taunted my husband? Did you think he would let

you get away with telling him you fucked his wife?"
She looked pissed as she tossed her purse next to the
door and threw her hands up.

"What did that jackass tell you? That isn't what I
said. Yeah, maybe I alluded to it, but–"

She cut me off, "Where the fuck do you get off
thinking you can *allude* to anything, Tyler? He's my
husband."

"He's a piece of shit who doesn't deserve you.
You *know* that! Sadie, what is going on? You're
acting completely different than you were last night.
Whatever he said, don't let him get to you. Don't let
this get to you." I motioned to my face, convinced she
was trying to push me away because she saw what
Scott had done. I stepped toward her, but she moved
back and held out her hand.

"Don't, Tyler. Don't make this harder on yourself." She looked annoyed with me as she crossed her
arms.

"Don't make *what* harder?" My breathing picked
up, and my body tensed in preparation for what it
assumed was coming next.

"I think you know. It's over. Last night showed
me that I let this thing between us go on for far too
long." She looked like she was having a normal,
everyday conversation, while my chest felt like it was
about to cave in.

"You're breaking up with me because of last
night?" I seethed.

"What can I say, Pup? You've outgrown your

kennel, and I don't like dealing with needy dogs. You showing up last night, trying to mark your territory, just reminded me you're too young, and that this has run its course." She motioned between us.

My heart dropped into my stomach at her words, and I searched her face for any crack in her armor. The Sadie standing in front of me was not *my* Sadie. Scott had to have gotten to her and said something to make her want to push me away.

"Stop it, Wifey. I know what you're doing," I spoke softly and tried to approach her again. She didn't move away this time and let me come closer until we were nearly chest-to-chest.

"You're trying to push me away because he threatened me, right? Well, look at me." I spread my arms out wide before gesturing down my body. "I'm alive, Sadie. And I can take care of myself."

"This isn't about that, Tyler. I'm sorry you got your ass handed to you, but you really should have thought about that before you tried to blow up my life. Scott did what he thought he needed to do to protect me," she sneered at me, and for the first time since I met her, I thought she looked ugly.

"Protect you? From what? Being happy? Why are you defending him? He treats you like shit! I treat you like a fucking goddess! I worship the ground you fucking walk on!"

"You can't give me what I want in life, Tyler! I don't want to give up my money! I don't want to give up the extravagant lifestyle I'm accustomed to. You can't provide for me the way he can!" she shouted.

"Is that really all you care about? I refuse to believe that you're just a materialistic woman, Sadie! You haven't cared about any of that down here!" I shouted back. My head started spinning, and I felt faint, but my anger fueled me.

She raised an eyebrow and barked a laugh. "Apparently, you haven't been paying attention, because that is who I've *always* been, Tyler. If you didn't pick up on that, it's because you didn't want to. You have this version of me in your head that you've built up, but guess what? I'm not your dream girl. I was having fun, and now I'm not. It's over."

She turned to leave, and I grabbed her elbow, wrenching her around to face me. "It's not fucking over. You're crazy if you think I'm letting you walk out of here like this. You *are* the woman I think you are. Something has you scared, and that's why you're acting this way. But it's fine. We love each other. We can-"

"I don't love you! I never loved you! Why do you think I didn't say it back last night? Or EVER? Don't you get it? This was just me giving in to your looks. You're hot, and I like riding your dick, but that's all. You're great to fuck, Tyler. But it was never anything more than that for me. You're not enough for me to be happy."

Letting go as if her skin burned me, I felt as

though she'd physically slapped me. My fists clenched at my sides as she narrowed her eyes.

"Sorry to disappoint you, Tyler. You should pay better attention to who you give your heart to." She bent to grab her purse and made it to the door just as I snapped.

My vision went red, and my body was tight with tension. I was in so much pain, physically and emotionally, but pushed it away as I stormed over and slammed the door just as she'd opened it. Pressing my weight into her, I caged her against the door and said, "If I'm so great to fuck, then do it, Sadie. You've already fucked me *over*. Now, fuck me one last time. I think you owe me that."

My lungs burned, and my breaths came in sharp puffs against her hair as I ground my semi-hard cock into her backside. She made a sound of protest but placed her hands flat against the door next to mine.

Her ass pushed back against me as she looked over her shoulder. "You want it one last time, Pup?"

"One time isn't going to get you out of my fucking system. Your touch is fucking branded on my goddamn bones. You've ruined me for any other woman who actually deserves me. But I *need* to have you one last time. So be the whore we both know you are and sit on my dick."

I fucking hated her at that moment. I hated how she'd made me feel. How, even though she was being a fucking bitch, I wanted nothing more than to bury my cock deep inside her. My harsh words were just that–only words. She hurt me, and I wanted to hurt her back.

Pulling her away from the door, I dragged her to the couch. She struggled against my grip on her arm, but her eyes shone with lust when I released her and turned to take off my sweatpants. She licked her lips and stared at my cock that was now jutting out, just waiting for her to envelop it in her sweet cunt. I quickly unbuttoned her jean shorts as she stood there, not moving to help me, but not resisting either. Yanking them down her hips, I sat on the couch, pulling her onto my lap.

She threw her head back with a moan as she sank on to me. I hissed as she started to roll her hips. The movement caused both pleasure and pain as she ran her hands down my bruised ribs before planting them on the back of the couch for leverage.

Thrusting into her as I squeezed her hips, my fingers clenched like I was trying to brand her skin. She cried out in pain and looked sharply at me with shock, but I didn't relent and continued to slam into her.

"This is what you wanted, right, Sadie? This is what I'm good for?"

Moving a hand to rub her clit, I didn't bother being gentle. She laughed as she rolled her head back and rode me faster. "This is exactly what you're good for."

My fingers pinched her in retaliation for her words, but instead of it being a punishment, she came with a cry. Her hips faltered as I squeezed harder, and she hissed in pain. Using all my strength, I stood, still buried inside her, and walked down the hall to my bedroom.

She leaned down to try and bite my lip, but I jerked my head back. "You're going to use that mouth for other things right now."

I dropped her unceremoniously onto my bed. As I ripped my cock from her pussy, it sprang up, glistening with her cum. Grabbing her legs, I spun her around, so her head hung off the side of my bed.

My knees bent as I shoved my cock into her open mouth. I also didn't give her time to adjust or get used to it, watching as her saliva spilled out the sides, and I burned the fucking image to my memory.

I could tell she was struggling to breathe from how hard I was fucking her mouth. Little noises that signaled she wasn't enjoying it as much as usual, were the only sounds in the room besides the sloppy wet ones of her sucking me off. But I couldn't bring myself to give a fuck.

Leaning over, I pushed my dick further down her throat, to spit on her pussy that was already gleaming with her earlier release. She jolted as I slapped her clit, and her teeth scraped lightly over my cock, catching me off guard and causing me to come.

She stared at me upside down as I stood, slowly pulling out so that just the tip was still in her mouth, and we both watched as my dick pulsed, raining my cum down her throat. Mascara tears ran black down her face. Lipstick was smeared around her mouth, and her breathing was labored.

For a moment, I was worried I'd actually hurt her.

Then I remembered her earlier words. *I don't love you. You're not enough.* And I let out a short laugh as I stepped back, my dick falling from her mouth, before turning to grab a pair of jeans from my dresser.

Sadie sat up and grabbed the sheet to cover herself while she wiped at her face. "Tyler-"

"Nah. I'm not interested in more of your bullshit, Sadie. This was just me wanting to get my dick wet one more time. That's what I'm good for, right?"

"Don't be cruel. It's not who you are," she whispered through soft tears. Her demeanor was different now, and my resolve almost crumbled, but she'd shown me the real her earlier, and I wouldn't be fooled again.

"Maybe it's how I should be from now on," I scoffed. "After all, that's what you're into, isn't it? An asshole who treats you like shit, fucks around on you, and gets lesser men to do his dirty work?"

Her eyes traveled over my face, taking in all the bruising, as I clenched my jaw and pulled a shirt over my head.

"Don't go."

Grabbing my wallet and keys off the dresser I turned to leave, pausing at the door. "Don't be here when I get back, Sadie. I'm sure we'll see each other around because of Chance and Rylee, but as far as I'm concerned, you're a stranger to me now."

Her muffled cries followed me as I walked through the house, but I refused to pause—the fear of changing my mind lingering as I slammed the door and got into my truck.

It was my fault. I'd let my guard down and thought I'd finally found someone who thought I was enough. Though it honestly didn't surprise me that I wasn't. I'd heard it before. Many times. But I would be damned if I stayed with her after she'd told me I was good for fucking and nothing else.

I had more respect for myself than that.

But it didn't change the fact that Sadie had ruined me. And this time, I didn't think I could save my heart from the fallout.

THE SECOND I HEARD TYLER'S TRUCK DRIVE away, I darted to the bathroom and relieved my stomach of its contents as tears continued to stream down my face. Trying to convince him that I thought he was good for nothing other than fucking was the hardest thing I'd ever had to do. And judging by his reaction, I'd say I put on a damn good show.

When my stomach was empty, I got up from where I sat on the floor and rinsed my mouth. Finding my clothes, I dressed and walked to my car, hiccups forming in my throat as I attempted to get my crying under control.

The sight of Tyler when he'd opened the door had caused my stomach to churn; at the same time, anger surged through my veins. Scott told me he would hurt Tyler unless I ended things, but he hadn't even given me a chance to break it off. I knew instantly, even before Tyler confirmed it, that Scott was responsible for his beaten and bruised body.

All I'd bring Tyler was trouble if we continued the way we had been, and I would never be able to forgive myself if something happened to his sister next. I'd gone there to talk everything out and figure out how to keep him and Ashlee safe, but the second he opened the door, I knew what I had to do.

I couldn't take any chances. So, I broke his heart—and mine.

How would I handle seeing him and not being *with* him. I knew I would never be able to stick around and watch as he moved on with someone else.

It was selfish. He deserved to be happy. But I wanted that happiness to be with *me*.

Feeling helpless and frustrated, a cold hollow sensation settled in my chest, as if Tyler had siphoned all the warmth from it when he walked out.

Slamming my palms against the steering wheel, I let out a long scream, feeling as lonely as when I'd first arrived in Jacksonville.

As though she'd known I needed her, Rylee's name flashed across the screen on my dashboard. Sucking in a deep breath I hit accept, but the moment her concerned voice came across the speakers, tears streamed down my face once more.

"Sadie, Tyler just showed up at our house and is *not* okay. What the hell happened in New York? He looks like he got the shit beat out of him!"

A horn sounded, and I swerved, my tears causing my vision to be so blurry I could barely see the road. I never cried, let alone sobbed like a baby. Part of me felt extremely foolish at what a mess I was. I'd always prided myself on staying calm and collected in stressful situations.

But I was losing my shit at the moment, and I didn't know how to find it again.

"Rylee," I blubbered. It was all I could manage without my face scrunching up, causing my view of the road to be completely obstructed.

"Oh, babe. Where are you? I'm on the way," her voice soothed.

"Home," I managed as I pulled into my complex's lot.

"Okay, I'll be there soon. It's gonna be okay."

As soon as the call disconnected, I got out of my car and managed to make it into my building without completely breaking down. *'You're not a fucking baby, knock it off and put your big girl pants on,'* I repeated in my head.

By the time I entered my condo and threw myself dramatically on the couch, my tears were slowly receding and had been reduced to the sad little huffs you get when you finish crying really hard.

Time seemed to pass in a blur. I don't know how long I'd been staring at the ceiling, lost in my thoughts, when Rylee let herself in and called out, "Sadie?"

"In here," I responded, shifting to sit up.

"What the hell happened between you two?" she asked, setting her purse on the counter, along with a plate of what looked like cupcakes.

"Bring those over here." My tone was watery as I waved her over.

"Obviously. I figured the situation was gonna need comfort food. And lots of wine." She pulled a bottle of rosé out of her purse, and I shook my head.

"Grab the vodka from the liquor cabinet. I need something stronger than wine."

"Oh, girl. I figured. This is for me. I only caught part of what Tyler said before Chance took him out on the patio, but he sounded rough. Chance was really worried. We thought he went to New York to tell you he loved you. What the fuck happened?"

She brought the cupcakes over, along with the vodka bottle and her pink wine that was just so utterly *Rylee*. As she grabbed glasses, I didn't bother to wait and ripped the plastic wrap off the plate, unwrapping the cupcakes and making little sandwiches out of them.

"Scott happened," I said around a mouthful of vanilla cake and chocolate frosting. "The whole thing was completely fucked, Ry. Tyler showed up at the gala and basically outed us, after I served Scott divorce papers before we'd even left for the party."

"Wait, you served Scott divorce papers? Sadie, I'm so proud of you. I know that must have been really hard for you," she said, reaching for a cupcake.

214

I frowned and pulled the plate away as she snatched one. "*I* need these, thank you very much."

Her eyes grew wide, and she laughed. "Sorry. Continue."

Starting on my second cupcake, I told the story. Everything, from giving Scott the papers and Tyler showing up at the gala, to finding out that he thought Scott was responsible for the death of his parents, and Scott saying it was his brother who did it.

"We were married at the time. *Married*, Rylee. Tyler was a child who lost his parents because of something my brother-in-law did, while I was still in the honeymoon phase of my marriage. Why do you think he kept that from me? I think that's something that Tyler should have told me right away! At least after we began sleeping together. Like, how am I supposed to believe it wasn't all some elaborate revenge plot?"

Rylee raised an eyebrow as she picked off part of her dessert and popped it into her mouth. "Do you really think that's what Tyler was doing?"

"No, not really. And I have no clue what he said to Scott when I walked away, but whatever it was, it was enough to send Scott into a fucking fury. That man has *never* laid a hand on me, and until last night, I would never believe he would try to harm me. But the bruises on my fucking jaw under all this makeup say otherwise, as does Tyler's whole fucking body. I'm so mad at him, Rylee. How could he do that?" I started to cry again and unwrapped a third cupcake.

"He told me I had to break things off, or he'd kill him. Then didn't even give me a chance to *do* it. When I showed up at Tyler's house, I was going to tell him everything. That I'd asked Scott for a divorce, and that he'd threatened him and Ashlee. But when I saw how badly his body was beaten, I just knew I had to end things. I can't, in good conscience, stay with him."

"He does look terrible. Didn't you say you have a really good lawyer?"

"It doesn't matter if I have a good lawyer. Scott said he would know if I didn't break it off with Tyler. What happens if he sends people down here after him? Or if he already has people here watching? A lawyer can't stop that. And Scott will always have someone else doing the dirty work and ensuring it can't be traced back to him. The thought of it makes me sick. All I could think of when I saw Tyler was, what happens next time? What if he doesn't survive another beating? And who wants to live like that? No one!" I cried before stuffing my mouth.

Drinking a mouthful straight from the bottle, I washed the sugared cake down with vodka. The combination instantly churned my stomach. Deciding against another one, I set the plate on the white, distressed, beach wood tray on my ottoman.

"I don't know, Sadie. I'm sure it was tough to find out that Scott knew his parents and that Tyler kept that from you this whole time, but I don't think he meant it maliciously. If anything, he was probably scared to tell you because he didn't want you to think of your relationship as revenge. But you two were really happy together. I've never seen you laugh like you do when you're with him. Don't you think that's worth a discussion about your future, instead of you making that decision on your own?" Rylee played devil's advocate.

My narrowed eyes slowly slid to hers, and she raised her hands in sync with her brows. "I just want you to be happy, babe."

"And I want to protect what makes me happy, Rylee. You don't understand my husband or our world up there. And I, very obviously, don't know him as well as I thought I did."

"So to keep Tyler and his sister safe, you're going to what, Sadie? Continue going back and forth and pretend like nothing ever happened? You two are going to run into each other. You're my maid-of-honor, and he's Chance's best man. Are you going to be able to walk down the aisle together and just pretend like it all meant nothing to you? You don't want to do that. I know you don't. There has to be another way. You can't just give up." Rylee sounded determined, and my heart warmed, knowing that my friend cared so much for my happiness.

"I hate to say this, but I need you not to say anything to Chance, Ry. I'm sorry, I feel so shitty for asking you to keep something from him, but you know he'll tell Tyler. And I can't risk this getting any more convoluted than it already has."

Her voice was soft as she, without hesitation, said a simple, "Okay."

I recalled Scott's threats about taking Sugar and Scotch and crushing her dreams. I couldn't–wouldn't–be responsible for that either. No, I had to deal with this alone. I had to deal with this carefully and subtly, so no one else got hurt.

But subtle had never been a Sadie Tailor strong suit.

"MRS. TAILOR, he's on a conference call. You can't go in there!" Scott's secretary yelled at me as I stormed past her desk.

Barely sparing her a glance, I continued my trek to Scott's office and spat, "Janet, I'm warning you, do NOT get in my way right now."

The older lady, who I had hand-picked myself for the job, gave an exasperated sigh as she stopped chasing me and returned to her desk. I heard her pick up the phone as if she were going to warn Scott that I was there, but a second later, the sound of it being placed back in its cradle reached my ears just as my hand landed on the doorknob.

Scott's gaze lifted as I walked in and slammed the door behind me. He looked annoyed as he hit a button on the phone on his desk, interrupting a man who was talking over the speaker. "I'm afraid I'm going to have to cut this call short. Something important just came up. We can resume this later."

Hitting another button, he picked up the receiver before quickly dropping it into the cradle again as I threw my purse down. His eyes found my angry glare as he leaned back in his chair while I stormed around his desk, the sound of my hand meeting his cheek echoing in the room a second later.

He clenched his jaw, and a scowl warped his handsome features. "To what do I owe the *pleasure*, dear wife? You're back from Florida early. Say all your goodbyes?"

"How *could* you?" My voice was firm even though my adrenaline was racing. My palm stung where it had struck his cheek, but the pain grounded me as I stared down at the man I once thought incapable of physically harming another person.

"You'll have to be a bit more specific, Sadie," he drawled.

He looked relaxed and unphased by my unexpected presence, and it stoked the raging fire that burned under my skin. "You had Tyler beaten! You told me to break things off with him, and I did! And while you were manhandling me at home, you hired men to send him a message. You said you wouldn't touch him if I ended things."

He laughed, and the sound spurred my fury. "I said no such thing. I told you to end things and that I would know if you didn't."

"Scott, you didn't even give me a chance!" I was about to hit him again, but stopped myself. Wondering at how easily I'd let him reduce me to a violent woman.

"You shouldn't have been fucking him in the first place, and none of this would have happened." He shrugged nonchalantly. His calm, relaxed demeanor irritated me, and I could feel the beginning of angry tears pricking my eyes.

The shrill ring of his desk phone startled me, and I jumped slightly. I knew Janet wouldn't be patching any calls through, so I wondered what was so important she felt the need to interrupt our argument.

"What will it take for you to leave him alone? I did what you asked. I went straight back to Jacksonville last weekend and ended things. I want you to leave him, and his sister, the fuck alone. Do you understand me, Scott?"

The phone rang again as he smirked. "I have a feeling we are starting to understand each other better. Now, we should discuss your moving back in."

A look of confusion crossed my face. "What do you mean? I never moved out."

"No, but you spend far too much time in Jacksonville. There's no reason for it. I want you here, by my side, where I know you won't get yourself into any more trouble."

Opening my mouth to reply, I was cut off by the door opening as Janet popped her head in. "Excuse me, Mr. Tailor, but Vinny Morroni is here to see you.

I told him he needed to make an appointment, but he said to tell you who he was and that you'd make time," she squeaked.

Scott's face melted into horrified surprise as his head snapped in her direction and he abruptly sat up. "Tell him I'm busy," he demanded curtly.

"I did. He said sending me was a courtesy, and if that were your response, he wouldn't be so polite again," she responded nervously.

I watched my husband gulp as he stood and buttoned his suit jacket. Whoever this Vinny Morroni was, he ruffled Scott's feathers. I couldn't remember a time when I had ever seen him look as nervous as he did right now. Even when he dealt with men he didn't like, he was always cool as a summer breeze on the water.

"Thank you, Janet. Send him in after a minute."

She left, shutting the door quietly behind her as Scott stepped into me. He reached out to grab my waist, and I startled in surprise. Starting to step back, his gaze cut to mine, and the uneasy look in his eyes made me freeze.

"I need you to listen to me very carefully. You need to act like we are a happily married couple right now. Do you understand me? Whatever happens, we are a united front. Do not say a word unless he speaks directly to you," he explained in a rush.

"Are you serious? What–"

"Sadie, there isn't time to explain. I need you to trust me." His voice dropped softer as he continued,

"I know that's probably hard for you to do right now. But I can't stress enough how important it is for us to look united."

My eyes bounced between his. His body was fraught with tension, and I realized...he was *scared*. I'd never known Scott to be scared of anything. Finally, I nodded, and he let go of me as I softly said, "Okay."

I'd barely perched myself on the edge of his desk before the door opened again, and two men walked in. Both were large and imposing, with dark hair and leathery skin that looked like they'd sunbathed for a week straight. One walked a few steps in front of the other, his face was greasy and pockmarked, and his large, reddish lips were turned down in a frown.

I assumed the other man was Vinny. His demeanor screamed *big* and *bad* in his beige suit, with an *I dare you* countenance. His hair was slicked back, and he had an unlit cigar in his mouth as he looked around Scott's office.

Vinny's eyes landed on me, and a giant smile spread across his face. He reached up to remove the cigar and gestured to me. "Scott, Scott, Scott. I have seen you with some very lovely ladies on your arm, but *this* is what you've been hiding at home? Shame on you. Such beauty deserves to be shown off."

If his name and appearance hadn't already told me he was Italian, his voice would have. I let out a sultry laugh. "Well, Mr. Morroni. Flattery will get you everywhere."

He laughed with me, and I could see Scott freeze out of the corner of my eye. He'd told me not to speak unless spoken to, but how could I let that compliment go unrewarded? You catch more flies with honey, after all.

"What can I do for you, Vinny? As you can see, I'm a little busy at the moment." For as scared as he looked a minute ago, Scott's voice had returned to its usual air of *I'm better than you.*

The smile dropped from the large man's lips, and his attention snapped to Scott. "I think you know why I'm here, Scotty. Your good friend, *the Senator*, decided to cut ties with me to bring you into the fold at the club. This is a problem, you see, because I have business at the club, and I don't appreciate being cut off from it so abruptly. Micky boy didn't even have the manners to sit down and discuss it with me. He sent his men to tell me my help was no longer needed. And I don't take too kindly to that."

"Whatever business you have with Mick is between you and him. I don't take kindly to you barging into my office and making threats," Scott's voice dripped with annoyance.

The air in the room shifted, and I heard the soft click of the safety being turned off before I realized I was staring down the barrel of a gun. Sucking in a breath, I pushed my body back and locked eyes with the man accompanying Vinny.

"*That's* a threat, Scotty. I didn't come here to make threats. I came here to get answers. I wanna know why Micky boy thought he needed to cut me out completely, instead of us all working together," Vinny explained as he lit his cigar smoothly as if they were discussing normal business.

The sweet, smoky aroma filled the room as Scott surged toward me and growled, "Get that fucking gun out of my wife's face. What the fuck, Vinny?"

He smacked the gun away, and I breathed out through my nose as I turned to glare at the Italian man who watched Scott through narrowed eyes. Scott turned and marched up to him, and multiple things happened simultaneously.

Vinny's eyes flicked over Scott's shoulder, and I was yanked off the desk by his henchman. My surprised yelp quickly turned to a soft gasp as the cold barrel of his gun pressed into my temple. Scott pivoted, and his eyes grew wide as Vinny laughed.

"Maybe this is the only way I can get you to talk, Scotty. Do I gotta have Joey over there rough up your pretty wife? This doesn't have to get ugly, but honestly, it's easier for us that way. Things get done quicker and easier when we use violence."

"Fuck you," I spat, struggling against Joey.

Pain burst across my cheek as he released his hold on me, and I fell to the floor with a cry. I wasn't entirely sure, but was fairly certain he'd hit me with the butt of the gun. Gingerly, I touched my cheek, wincing at the bruise I was sure was forming under the knot I now felt, and looked up to see Scott rush at Joey. The man chuckled as he sidestepped and walked over to Vinny, who watched us with thinly veiled aggravation.

"I will fucking kill you. Do you hear me? Consider your man dead, Vinny. And get the fuck out of my office," Scott shouted as he helped me up.

Vinny hmphed and pursed his lips. "Sorry to mar that beautiful face, Mrs. Tailor. Scotty, we'll be in touch. Hopefully, you'll be ready to talk more seriously then."

"I'm serious now, Vinny. I want my pound of flesh before I talk about anything," Scott stated as he touched my cheek lightly. His gaze bore into mine, regret shining clear in his eyes.

Vinny scoffed, "It's just a scratch. She'll be fine."

Scott twisted to look over his shoulder. I wasn't sure what Vinny saw on his face, but eventually, the man conceded a nod. "You'll get your pound of flesh. Have your secretary put a meeting on the books."

Joey scowled at us as Vinny turned to leave. Before they walked out the door, Scott demanded, "I want to collect it myself."

Vinny paused for a moment and only gave a nod as his answer before he disappeared, leaving a cloud of smoke in his wake. Joey slammed the door behind him, and I let out a strangled cry as I sank into Scott's arms.

"Sadie, I'm so fucking sorry. I told you not to say anything."

"What the fuck have you gotten yourself into,

Scott?" I cried, holding a palm to my cheek to soothe the sting.

He helped me into a chair and picked up the phone on his desk. "Janet, can you please bring me some ice wrapped in a towel?"

She appeared a few minutes later, the silence between us as thick as the residual scent of the Cuban Vinny had lit up. Janet handed me the ice with a sympathetic look, and I nodded my thanks as I pressed the cool compress to my face.

Once she was gone, Scott turned from where he'd moved to look out the floor-to-ceiling window that offered him a gorgeous view of Central Park. I didn't know what to say and was too lost in my thoughts to move.

"Mick made a mistake, and now I'm paying for it."

"No fucking shit," I spat. My hand that held the ice dropped to my lap as I glared at my husband. "Who the fuck *are* you?"

He had the grace to look ashamed, and let out a big sigh as he unbuttoned his suit jacket, sinking back into his chair. He massaged his temple with two fingers before sliding them under his chin as he propped his elbow on the arm.

"I think it's time we had a long talk."

All I'd ever wanted was for Scott to include me in his life outside of our marriage. I wanted to know about his business deals and his companies, and once, I'd even offered to work at any department he'd set me up at—so that I could be closer to him. But that was years ago, back when I still craved his attention and approval.

Now? Now, I had a feeling that whatever he was about to tell me, I didn't want anything to do with.

And something told me that, for once, I was better off not knowing.

CHAPTER NINETEEN

Tyler

THE CRISP NOVEMBER AIR OF CHICAGO FILLED my lungs as I followed Ashlee and her friends into their favorite bar. It had been two weeks since I left Sadie in my bed and told her not to be there when I returned.

I hadn't seen her since.

There was a Sadie-sized chasm where my heart was supposed to be, and I had no idea how to fill it. After spending the first week shuffling between my couch and bed, refusing to go to work or even shower, Chance called my sister and told her I needed to get out of Florida for a little while.

Ashlee had been ecstatic. It'd been over a year since I'd been the one to visit her, and I had to admit that I'd kind of missed The Windy City.

Her friends, not so much.

Maybe it was that the only females I'd spent time with were Sadie and Rylee for the better part of the last seven and a half months. Did they get drunk and all squealy? Yeah, sometimes. But it was a whole different story with the flock of women my sister's age.

They'd gone straight to the bar for shots and then to the dance floor, where they were all whooping and hollering–Ashlee included.

I sat on a stool, catty-corner from a tall guy with sandy blond hair who was covered in tattoos. He watched the girl behind the bar intensely as he chewed the toothpick in his mouth–though he looked like he'd rather be chewing on her instead.

Said bartender came up with a smile as she set a napkin and a beer down on the bar top in front of me. "So, you're the infamous Tyler. Ashlee's told us all about you. Nice to finally meet you."

She had long glossy black hair that was tied up in a ponytail and dark chocolate eyes that scrutinized me as I looked at the beer with a raised brow. "Your sister ordered it for you. Though you look like you could use something a bit stronger? You look like you just lost your best friend."

"You could say that. I'll take a Jameson, neat, please," I muttered and shrugged out of my jacket.

"I'm Jess, and this is Sean. We're good listeners if you need someone to talk to. Something tells me you won't be joining Ashlee and her friends on the dance floor," Jess said as she poured me a double and nodded her head in the tattooed man's direction. He was now watching our interaction closely, and I had a hard time gauging their relationship.

"You seem to know my sister pretty well," I stated before taking a sip of my single malt scotch.

"Sean and I are good friends with her boss, Daphne. Ash started coming in with them about half a year ago. She's got a good head on her shoulders. You should be proud," Jess explained before moving to help another customer.

I must have looked as confused as I felt, because Sean leaned on the bar and said, "Ashlee says you basically raised her after your parents died." His words were slow, and his voice had a low rasp to it.

"That's not true. Our maternal grandmother took us in," I told him.

He shrugged. "Well, your sister thinks very highly of you. She's been worried about your well-being with everything that's been going on."

Why was Ashlee telling these people my life story?

Sean laughed and drank the rest of whatever was in his glass. Jess returned a moment later and filled it with club soda, then gave him another one filled with limes.

"Relax," she said, "we aren't going to judge you. Love is love. It doesn't matter if you're a man or a woman. A they or them. Younger or older...as long as you're of legal age. And as long as everyone consents. You fell in love with a woman who's twenty years older than you.

So what? She's married, and her husband sounds like a real piece of work, but that's okay. This is a safe space. Ashlee said you haven't felt like you can really talk about it because you guys share the same best friends. Well, you don't know us, even though we know quite a bit about you. You can talk it all out here if you want."

What the fuck, Ashlee?

"Talk what out?" My sister sounded out of breath as she appeared on my right.

My head slowly turned to her, and I narrowed my eyes. "Why are you telling people about what's going on with me and Sadie?"

"*Is* there a you and Sadie still? Cause you won't talk to me about it. Chance and Rylee said you haven't talked to them either, and that's the end of your friend list, bro." She took the shot that Jess had placed in front of her and shrugged before bounding off to rejoin her friends.

"Ash said she used to be a model, so we totally got curious and looked your Sadie up. Good job, man. She's a bonafide hottie," Jess complimented.

A smirk pulled at my lips, and I couldn't help it. Shaking my head, I placed my elbows on the bar, running my hands up my face and through my hair as I sighed. "Yeah, she is."

Fuck, I miss her.

"So, what's the problem? Besides the fact that she's married. The dude sounds like a total douchebag, by the way. We looked him up, too, as soon as one of the articles mentioned who her husband was."

"Jess really likes Google. She probably knows more about your girl than you do," Sean spoke around his toothpick.

"I doubt that." I laughed into my drink.

I knew Sadie inside and out better than anyone. Or, at least, I liked to think that I did. I wanted to believe she pushed me away and said all those hurtful things because she thought she was protecting me. But the *way* she said them...she knew right where it would hurt me.

And she had *wanted* to hurt me.

Something slammed on the bar before me, pulling me from my reverie. "Bet," Jess said with a smirk, her hand around a bottle of Jameson.

"Here we go. Jess also really likes her drinking games," Sean mumbled under his breath.

Leaning forward on my stool, I pushed my glass away and pulled the Jameson between us. "You're on."

"Last name—" she asked.

"Tailor, duh. Drink up," I responded imme-diately.

"You didn't let me finish. Last name *before* she got married."

Thinking about it briefly I was struck with the realization I had no idea.

Well, shit.

Jess smirked and raised a brow as she poured the amber-colored liquid into my shot glass. "St. James.

I'll take one too, though, since you thought my question meant current name."

We took our shots together and slammed them down simultaneously before she asked her next question. "Where did she grow up?"

I took a long breath, realizing we'd never discussed her childhood. I'd never wanted to bring up mine, so I'd avoided asking her anything about hers so she wouldn't dig into my past. "Fuck."

"All over. She was in and out of foster care from when she was twelve until she phased out." Jess poured me another shot, and I took it with no hesitation.

The fact I didn't know that about Sadie hit like a physical blow to the gut. That was some deep shit. Some potentially traumatizing shit. It made more sense now why she stayed with Scott for so long.

He was the security she never had growing up.

The chasm in my chest grew bigger with every question, and I registered I hadn't really tried to get to know Sadie at all. I knew her quirks and small things, but I didn't know *her*.

"Favorite drink."

A half smile pulled at my lips as I reached for the bottle. "Dirty vodka martini. Stirred, not shaken."

Jess took her shot before her attention turned to some guys on the other side of the bar. She held up a finger. "Hold that thought. You can ask the next question."

"She'll play this game with you until you're annihilated and don't remember your own name, let alone anything about your girl," Sean warned.

"I have a high tolerance." I nodded to his club soda. "Do you not drink?"

He shook his head. "Nah, not anymore. I did a stint in rehab a while back, hurt a friend, and realized I had a problem. It's under control now, and I probably could, but Jess has enough fun for the both of us."

These people that Ash had found for friends were really open about personal lives.

Before I could ask about the nature of their relationship, Jess returned and slapped the space between our empty shot glasses. "Next question!"

I didn't miss a beat and smirked. "Favorite sexual position?"

Jess looked smug as she answered confidently, "The Flatiron."

"What the fuck?" I looked at her incredulously. "How do you know that?"

"Dude, she did a spread for Playboy, and it was one of their questions. Drink up." She pushed my shot toward me.

How did I forget that? I reached out and took a deep breath. My eyes found Sean's as he grinned and shrugged as if to say, '*I told you so.*'

The whiskey was smooth as it went down my throat. I had a feeling it was going to be a long night, but I realized I didn't care. I was kind of having fun for the first time in a while.

And at least I was in good company.

Even if it was proving that I never really knew Sadie at all.... That fault was entirely mine.

MY HEAD POUNDED as sunlight suddenly streamed into the room, directly into my face. I winced and held a hand up in an attempt to block out the sun. A girlish giggle that did not sound like my sister came from my left, and my head whipped in that direction, causing a sharp bolt of pain to stab my brain.

What the fuck did I do last night?

"Wakey, wakey, eggs and bakey," the girl said.

Everything was foggy as I slowly sat up. Once out of direct sunlight, I could make out Jess sitting cross-legged on a coffee table in front of me. She was wearing pajama shorts and an oversized t-shirt that fell off one shoulder, and was holding out a steaming mug of coffee.

"Where am I?" I croaked out as I took it. My mouth felt like I'd slept in a desert, and I was grateful for the liquid gold that instantly started to chase my headache away.

"My place. I Airbnb it out now, but there was a lull in reservations, and it's closer to the bar," she explained as she picked up another mug beside her. Her coffee looked lighter and had a faint sweet aroma drifting from it.

236

Nodding, I took another sip before I froze. Her hair was mussed, and I was shirtless. And where were my pants? I was in my boxers. Why wasn't I wearing my pants?

"Please tell me...we didn't...did we?"

Her face lit up as she laughed and shook her head vigorously. "Oh God, no! He would have killed you if you tried."

She jerked her thumb, and I looked over to see Sean sitting on a loveseat to the right of the couch I'd been lying on. He was fully dressed and smirking as he sipped his own mug of coffee. "Morning, sunshine. I told you she'd drink you under the table."

"Ashlee tried to get you to go home with her when she and her friends left, but you had a lot of stuff to get off your chest last night, my friend. I hope you feel better about the situation now," Jess said nonchalantly.

Vaguely, I recalled Ashlee trying to get me to leave and drunkenly refusing. Which was embarrassing as fuck, because no one liked the sloppy drunk guy at the bar. "Shit. Please tell me I didn't make an ass out of myself?"

"You didn't make an ass out of yourself. But I'll bet you can't remember anything we talked about, can you?" Sean asked as he stretched out and kicked his feet up on the coffee table.

Jess uncrossed her legs and went to sit beside him, cuddling into his side as he put his arm around her. As I watched them, I felt nostalgic. Sadie and I used to cuddle like that in the morning.

"I wish I could, but yeah, right now, I can't remember a damn thing." Placing my cup on the coffee table, I pulled over a magazine to act as a coaster, before falling back on the couch and grinding the heels of my palms into my eyes.

"Want me to sum it up for you?" Jess offered.

A brief thought flashed through my mind at how much Ashlee must trust these people to have left me with them all night. I couldn't remember a time, besides when I first met Chance and again with Sadie and Rylee, when I felt so comfortable talking to strangers. These two had offered their ears, their advice, and their home to me—no questions asked. The fact that I was Ashlee's brother was enough for them.

It made me feel at ease to know that my sister had surrounded herself with such great people.

Jess took my silence as a yes and began recalling the events of the night before. "Okay, well. We found out that you didn't know your girlfriend as well as you thought you did, but that's entirely because you didn't ask her anything about her life in case she asked you about yours in return. We worked out that Ashlee is *not* a fan of her, but she's willing to try, even though she's currently upset you didn't tell her that Sadie's husband had you beaten up."

"Yeah, have fun with that one when you get back

to her place. She also called your friend and yelled at him for not telling her," Sean cut in.

Jess nodded. "That, too. You told us all the awful things Sadie said, but honestly, that's just *classic* trying to push you away to protect you. It sounds like they are some pretty powerful people in New York, so I get her concern, but at the same time, you love each other–"

"She doesn't love me. She said so herself," I spat dejectedly, popping an arm between my head and the pillow as I looked over in time to see them share a knowing look. "What?"

"She threw you a birthday party and got you a Ninja Turtle costume," Sean said pointedly.

"Dressed up in your favorite modeling outfit of hers and sang you Happy Birthday," Jess chimed in.

"Held off on fucking you for months because she was worried about your feelings," Sean remarked.

"Is that what I told you?" I interjected.

"No, that part was just obvious. Was that not obvious to you?" Jess snorted.

"She held off on fucking me because she didn't want to be a cheater." Sitting up again, I looked around for my clothes.

"That may be true, but it sounded to me like she was also trying to be careful about your feelings. Even though you told her it didn't matter if she stayed married. She must really care about you, 'cause it must have been hell trying to keep you at arm's length." Jess' eyes traveled down my torso before she pointed behind me.

I twisted around to see my clothes folded on a little table behind the arm of the couch. My eyes flitted back over to Sean, who I assumed would not appreciate his girlfriend's comment, but he looked at me appreciatively as well, making me think that they were into some pretty interesting kinks.

"I really did word vomit last night, didn't I?" My head swam as I stood to get dressed, and took a minute to let the brain fog clear before I grabbed my pants.

"It probably felt good to get it all off your chest," Sean pointed out.

"Does it count if I can't remember it?" I snorted. However, I did feel lighter in a weird way that I couldn't explain. These last two weeks, I'd felt cold and detached from everything. Now, I felt a little more like myself.

Ashlee had texted me multiple times asking if I was up yet and wanted to meet her for brunch. Apparently, she wasn't worried at all about leaving me with people I didn't know. My stomach rumbled as I sent off a reply, telling her where I was and to come get me. After I dropped her a pin for my location, I turned back to my new friends.

Were we friends? They were playing footsies while looking like they wanted to eat me.

"Well, this has been fun. Thank you for taking care of me. Ashlee is on her way to get me." I pulled my shirt over my head, wishing I could remember the rest of last night. As my brain fog kept clearing, though, I was pretty sure I'd cried at some point and remembered Sean patting my back.

"Do you guys wanna go with us to get food?" I asked them. But they now looked like they wanted to eat each other.

"Nah, we're good. Thank you, though. Next time you're in town, you better stop by and say hello. Better bring Sadie with you, too," Jess said suggestively, with a waggle of her brows.

I sniffed. "What makes you think Sadie will be with me next time I'm in town?"

Jess and Sean both stood, and she took me by surprise as she reached out to embrace me. "Oh, Tyler. You're not going to let her slip through your fingers. You guys might need some time apart right now, but you love her too much to let her go. This guy took over a year to figure his shit out." She nodded at Sean. "You'll figure it out, too."

For some reason, I believed her.

CHAPTER TWENTY

ONE WHOLE MONTH WITHOUT TYLER, AND I WAS beginning to think I should just return to New York permanently. I felt like I was sharing custody of Chance and Rylee with an estranged husband who was nowhere to be found.

Speaking of husbands, Scott had started to unnerve me with how nice he was being.

After the incident with Morroni, it was like Scott did a complete one-eighty and reverted back into a doting husband.

But I didn't want to be doted on. Not by him.

I just wanted my pup back.

Scott knew I was miserable, too. He even arranged for me to bring Rylee to Vera Wang in a few weeks for a custom wedding gown, thinking it would make me happy to give my friend such an extravagant gift.

She and I both scoffed at his offer but later agreed because, *Vera Wang*.

You don't look a gift horse in the mouth.

It wasn't *my week* to do something with Chance and Rylee, so I wasn't entirely sure what I was even doing in Jacksonville. Riya had completely taken over my position at the bar, besides doing the books.

I wasn't really needed here anymore, and I'd thought about bringing it up to Rylee soon.

Recently, I'd entertained a few different realtors representing clients who were looking in the area, allowing them to come by to look at my condo.

Jacksonville didn't feel like home anymore. In fact, it almost felt like as much of a prison as New York.

I couldn't go anywhere without fear of running into Tyler. Though Scott was singing a different tune these days, I wouldn't put it past him to still have eyes on me. And I wouldn't want whoever was watching me to report back to him that I saw Tyler, even if it was just at the bar when he showed up for work.

And God forbid I saw him with another woman. I'd probably just curl up and die on the spot.

So many times, I wanted to rush over to his house and tell him I didn't mean any of it. Wanted to tell him I loved him, that I missed him. And even though I'd used it as a means to hurt him, I really missed fucking him.

An entire month of no sex was enough to drive me bananas.

A knock on the door pulled me from my spot on the balcony. I'd been spending more and more time on the beach, reflecting on life and what exactly I wanted from the rest of mine. I'd been waiting for the knock. It was an important day for me and Scott, not that I really cared anymore, but I *was* expecting some lavish gift or a large bouquet of roses.

What I was not expecting was to open the door and see my husband himself, accompanied by the little old lady that lived in the condo below mine. My eyes widened in shock as I took in Scott, wearing a pair of dark gray shorts and a lighter gray t-shirt, arm in arm, with Mrs. Waverly.

"You sure know how to pick them, honey. I was just asking this hottie here if he was sure he wanted to come up to your place when he could come down to mine. Told him I could probably teach him a thing or two," she rasped in her throaty tone.

Leaning against the doorframe, I crossed my arms, smirking as I said, "By all means, take him if you want him."

"Hey, now. Do I get a say in this?" Scott joked.

"Betty! You can't just disappear like that!" Marjorie, Mrs. Waverly's nurse, shouted from the end of the hall. Betty jumped, and we all watched as Marjorie marched toward us, a stern look on her face.

"Shit. I better go before she has an aneurysm.

Scott, my offer still stands if you want to stop by later." She let go of Scott's arm with a wink and turned to start hobbling away, her cotton candy pink hair flowing in the slight breeze.

As I watched her go, I shook my head. "Unbelievable."

"She's fun," he simply stated as I moved out of the way and allowed him to enter.

"What are you doing here?" I asked, shutting the door.

"I wanted to see you today. Happy anniversary, by the way. How is it that I've never seen this place?"

As he turned back to face me, I saw a manila envelope in his hand that I hadn't noticed before, and my heart skipped a beat. "Honestly, I've never wanted you here. And you've never cared to come down before."

He had the grace to look remorseful as he softly replied, "I know."

"So, do you want the tour?"

Grimacing, he looked around. "Probably not, now that I think of it. Is there a safe place to sit that hasn't been contaminated by the kid?"

I smirked and moved to sit on the couch. "Nope. We fucked on just about every surface here. Pick a place and deal with it."

"Classy," he deadpanned, but took a seat on the couch, leaving a cushion of space between us. He tossed the envelope on the ottoman before kicking a

246

foot over his knee as he put an arm over the back of the couch.

"I'm here to give you what you want." He gestured to the ottoman. "It's all there, except I had it corrected. Your lawyer signed off on it."

I bristled, caught between surprise and acute anger. "What are you talking about?"

"I've had a while to think about it, and I've decided to give you a divorce. You're miserable, Sadie. And frankly, I don't think Vinny Morroni will be a problem any longer, so I don't feel like I need to protect you anymore. Or, at least, protect you by staying married to you. It didn't exactly work out the way I thought it would."

Confusion wormed through my brain as I tried to piece together everything he'd said. "I don't understand."

Letting out a long sigh, he stood from the couch and put his hands in his pockets as he went to stare out the large window that overlooked the beach. "I know I haven't been a good husband to you. I haven't been for a while. And honestly, when you bought this place and met Rylee, I saw the light in you I'd snuffed out a long time ago come back to life. I didn't realize the shit Mick was getting me into because I trusted him. When Vinny started making threats, I panicked. You don't fuck with the Mafia and get away with it.

"Luckily, it wasn't hard to dig up dirt on Morroni, and Mick has the feds in his pocket. When he barged into my office and his man put his hands on you?" He didn't finish his sentence, and I could see from where I sat that his face was flushed in anger, and he was clenching his jaw.

"What did it mean when you said you wanted your pound of flesh?" I was pretty sure I knew the answer, but I was curious, and a small sick part of me wanted to hear Scott say it.

He turned and slowly made his way back to where he was sitting before. "I killed him," he answered simply.

"And then I showed Vinny the footage of him conducting his business and threatened to give it to the feds. He didn't really care about that because he's got guys in his pocket, too. But then I threatened to show the footage of him with some of the girls to his wife, Francesca. He loves that woman as much as I love you, and he'd do anything to keep her at his side. He also knows she'd kill him if she ever found out."

"Why didn't I think of that?" I muttered in amusement. Scott gave me a pointed look, and I smiled in return. "Kidding."

"So, you killed his guy? Joey? The thought of that should terrify me, but instead, I feel oddly avenged."

Fuck that guy.

Scott nodded. "And I realized that you were better off without me. Keep the last name if you want. If you want to change it back to St. James, we'll go through the proper channels to fix all the other paperwork."

"What other paperwork?"

"You're getting everything you're entitled to, Sadie. Half of our assets. Alimony. And then some. And when I die, you will remain my beneficiary, along with what we agreed to leave to Jackson."

My breath caught in my throat. Why was he doing this for me? Why now?

I hadn't realized I'd voiced my questions out loud until he answered, "Because I love you. And it's time to let you go."

His admission jarred me. "Just like that? After this entire time of fighting me, you're just giving up now?"

"Do you want me to continue fighting for you?"

I didn't say anything as a small smile crept over his face, and he looked at the cushion between us. "I didn't think so. I just realized that life is short, Sadie. You can be here one moment and gone the next. And I'd hate to think I forced you to spend your last moments chained to me."

"Well, that's ominous. Sounds more like you're going to have me offed."

He laughed and shook his head. "That's not what I meant, and you know it. The kid made you happy. I saw how you two looked at each other on the dance floor at the gala. Even behind the mask, he looked at you like you hung the moon."

"You knew it was him?"

"I did once he took his mask off at the bar. I watched him watch you for the rest of the night until he went up to Weylan. I knew in my gut something was up, but didn't piece it together until we were introduced. And I didn't realize how much it would hurt...to find out that you'd found someone else to make you happy. I know you hate me right now, but it doesn't even come close to how much I hate myself for hurting you. And for allowing you to get hurt. Especially when there is someone out there who would do anything to make sure you were never hurt again."

"It's not like that anymore, Scott. I did a damn good job convincing him I *didn't* love him. Not everything you break can be fixed again. Not everything you love comes back when you let it go. Sometimes, we don't get a happy ending." I shrugged as tears pricked my eyes and hastily wiped them away before they could fall.

Scott just smiled at me and shook his head. "You always were a great actress. It's a wonder you never went into film."

He stood and pressed a chaste kiss to my forehead. As he headed toward the door, I got up from the couch and followed him, startled as he turned so suddenly that we ran into each other. His hands came up to my arms to brace me, and we shared a chuckle.

"You know, you're just as stubborn as I am sometimes. Maybe you should be the one to reach out and apologize first."

Staring up at him incredulously, I asked, "Who *are* you? And what have you done with the real Scott Tailor?"

"I've been getting some good advice lately." He smirked, and he didn't have to tell me where he was getting said advice from. I just *knew*.

"So, one of your club girls told you to come down here and apologize?" There was no spark of jealousy or even annoyance. It actually kind of comforted me now, knowing that he had someone to talk to.

"I think you'd like her. Really, you would. She'd be a great match for Jackson."

I laughed. "Please don't subject the poor girl to the playboy ways of our nephew. And stop talking like you're going to arrange a marriage for him, for heaven's sake."

As my laughter died, Scott reached up and cupped my cheek lightly before pressing a light kiss to my lips. "I'm going to miss you, Sadie."

Nostalgia ran through me. Emotions I hadn't expected to feel rose to the surface and swirled in my chest. With a sad smile, I replied, "I know, Scott."

His hand slid down to interlace with mine, and I squeezed it lightly. "Thank you."

Turning to the door, his hand slipped away as he smiled softly and said, "Goodbye, Sadie."

And just like that, our divorce was finalized on the afternoon of our twentieth wedding anniversary.

CHAPTER TWENTY-ONE

Tyler

I'd sort of taken Jess' advice that things would work themselves out, but I realized that in order for that to happen, I needed to think about a lot of things. I needed time to process everything that had happened in the past few months.

A month had passed since my time in Chicago, making it six weeks since I'd seen Sadie. Well, six weeks since I'd talked to her, anyway. I'd seen her around town and through the windows of Sugar and Scotch. I knew I wasn't fooling Chance or any of the guys who worked for us when I put myself on the schedule for the bar's maintenance.

But I'd really wanted to *see* her, even if it meant hiding in the next aisle over at the grocery store. Or making sure she didn't notice me at the bar–thank you, Rylee.

From what I could tell, she looked happy. And I didn't know whether that fact bothered me or put me at ease. I'd gone through our last conversation at my house so many times. Picked apart every interaction we'd ever had, trying to figure out who the real Sadie was. Trying to figure out if I should fight for her or if she truly was happy being with her husband.

I'd gotten back into my pre-Sadie routine. A swim every morning. Clean the house every Wednesday. Laundry on Friday. Except now, I got every other week to hang out with Chance and Rylee. Our friends had decided on the shared custody agreement without our knowledge or consent.

Ironically, it was as though Sadie and I had gotten a divorce.

Sighing, I picked up a pillow from the floor in my bedroom. The giant collection I had amassed while we'd been together was no longer needed, so every night I threw them all off the bed until I was down to the original two I'd always slept with before.

As I leaned over to arrange them against the headboard, my foot kicked one underneath the bed. Crouching down, I grimaced and realized I needed to add vacuuming to my to-do list.

Pulling the pillow back out, a few familiar pearls rolled past me, and I grabbed them before they could get too far. Staring down at the cream beads in my palm, I realized they were the only bit of Sadie I had left, aside from my memories.

My thoughts drifted as I sat back on my heels. The night of my birthday was when everything changed. I should have told Sadie I loved her right then—when we were wrapped so deep in each other, I wasn't sure where I ended, and she began.

"Ty? Where you at, man?" Chance's voice pulled my attention to my open door, where he appeared a few seconds later.

"Hey, what are you doing here? I thought it wasn't *my week?*"

Chance rolled his eyes as he leaned against the frame. "Don't start with that again. Sadie took Rylee to New York to go wedding dress shopping. I wish you two would just spend a week in bed and fuck it out. You're both miserable. I know the wedding is still three and a half months away, but damn, Tyler. If you guys don't work your shit out, Rylee is going to murder you both if she thinks you guys will cause a scene."

"Yeah, because getting over someone you're in love with, who clearly told you they didn't love you back, is so easy," I muttered and moved to stand. "Thanks, Chance."

I counted to ten in my head as I pushed past him and made my way to the kitchen, the pearls still clutched in my hand. Ashlee suggested I try it when I got deep into my feelings and felt like I was starting to spiral. So far, it'd been working.

Right now, however, it wasn't.

Anger seeped into my bones, and I clenched my jaw as I heard Chance's footsteps behind me.

"You know that's bullshit, right? She loves you.

And now that Scott divorced her, you two are free to do whatever you want. I don't understand why you're not together when you both clearly want to be," Chance said, as if I'd already known the bomb he had just dropped.

My brows knit together as I spun around and asked, "What do you mean Scott divorced her?"

He looked at me incredulously before throwing his hands up in the air. "I *can't* with you guys."

"What did *I* do? I have no clue what you're talking about. When did this happen?" I clutched the pearls tighter and watched him walk to the kitchen to pull two bottles of Stella from the fridge.

My heart was doing backflips, and my chest began to ache as I waited for him to remove the caps off the green glass bottles before he motioned for me to sit on the couch with him. Instead, I took the Stella and sat on the loveseat to the left of the couch.

"Two weeks ago," he finally replied. "Showed up out of nowhere and just handed over the paperwork she'd given him before the gala."

What the fuck?

Sadie had given Scott divorce papers before the gala? Why hadn't she told me? Why the fuck didn't Rylee or Chance say anything?

"You knew about this and didn't say anything to me?" My tone sounded as betrayed as I felt, and Chance looked at me pointedly.

"*This* is why I can't handle you three. Everything is all *secrets this*, and *don't say anything that*. How about we start practicing this normal thing called *communication* so there's no more *misunderstandings*," he chastised and spoke slowly like I was a child. He took a drink of his beer and settled into the couch as he shook his head.

"I'm about to come over there and punch you in the face. How's that for misunderstandings? Did Sadie tell you guys not to tell me?" I wasn't in the mood to drink and set the bottle down on the coffee table.

I deliberately didn't use a coaster because I had been trying to break all my *Sadie habits,* but my knee started to bounce as I stared at the condensation while it dripped onto the glass. After barely twenty seconds, I lunged forward to grab one from the center of the table and set the bottle on it.

"Honestly, Ty. I thought you knew and were just being stubborn. I figured Sadie would have told you the second it happened. But Rylee has had a hunch that she's been thinking about moving back to New York, even with the divorce. Apparently, Scott told her she could have the penthouse if she wanted it. That's where the girls are staying while they're there," Chance explained as he pulled out his phone and checked it before tossing it on the cushion beside him.

My stomach felt like a rock had been dropped into it. "Why does Rylee think that?"

Chance shrugged. "Sadie's been really melancholy lately. If she hasn't told you, then maybe she's trying to figure out how to deal with her guilt. She was real torn up after Scott had you beaten. Riya pretty much took over her job at Sugar and Scotch. Maybe she feels like she's just not needed around here anymore? Rylee had a feeling she might bring it up while they're up there, but I just checked, and Ry hasn't said anything."

Sadie's words from our last encounter played in my head like a broken record. A panicked feeling settled in my chest at the thought of Sadie moving back to New York. Why would she want to be there instead of here, where her friends and business were? Especially if Scott had granted her a divorce.

"I think she's also worried that she'll have to watch you move on with someone else. Which wouldn't be a problem if you two just *talked* to one another. I swear you're both stubborn as mules," Chance continued.

"Okay, Mr. Wallowed in self-pity and every Glen ever made when Rylee pushed him away," I responded.

My mind was reeling with questions as to why Sadie hadn't said anything to me about her divorce. Especially if there was any truth to what Chance was saying about her being worried about me moving on. Surely she knew that there *was* no one else for me.

Whether I knew the real Sadie or not, it had only ever been her.

Everything that had happened in my past was to prepare me for Sadie Tailor.

Now I guess the only question was whether she was ready for me? But she sure as hell wouldn't be able to figure that out if she wasn't speaking to me.

"Rylee will do her best to convince her not to leave, right?" I leaned forward and picked up my beer to take a drink as Chance shot me a sly grin.

"Obviously. Sadie is her best friend. What's going on in that head of yours? You look like you have something planned. You look like yourself again."

"For the first time in a long time, I feel like myself again. And, obvious or not, make sure Rylee convinces Sadie to stay here."

CHAPTER TWENTY-TWO

As I waited for Rylee to step out of the dressing room at Vera Wang, I settled back into the black leather couch with a glass of champagne—my thoughts occupied with the conversation I had with Scott two weeks ago.

Him telling me to apologize to Tyler first had perplexed me.

Did I have things to apologize for? Absolutely.

But there were so many other things to factor in.

Sure, Scott said Vinny Morroni wasn't an issue any longer, but how could I believe that? He was the head of one of the families that ran the Italian Mafia. I'd done my research after that awful day in Scott's office. Back when I thought I'd be chained to him and would have to deal with whatever mess he'd gotten himself into with Mick.

Did Scott really think some blackmail footage of him with escorts would stop him from lashing out? I didn't want to risk Tyler getting caught up in that, but on the other side of the coin, was I going to spend the rest of my life looking over my shoulder, wondering if something would happen to *me*?

Scott had assured me that I was safe, and I wanted to trust him. At least in this particular situation.

And Tyler seemed to be doing just fine without me. I'd driven by him a few times as he was out working, and once, I'd walked into a restaurant to pick up takeout, only to see him there with some of the guys from work. I'd also almost *literally* run into him at the grocery store one time, but I panicked and shoved my cart full of snacks into the next aisle and left.

I'd really been craving those salt and vinegar chips too.

He appeared to be carrying on like everything was normal. I hadn't heard from him since the divorce, and I'd assumed Chance and Rylee would have told him... But, then again, why *would* he reach out after all the horrible things I said?

I set my champagne down to fish my phone from my purse. It wasn't that hard. All I needed to do was open my messages, type in Pup, then *I miss you*, and hit send.

There.

Done.

Wait.

Shit!

I wasn't supposed to actually send that.

The door to the fitting room opened, and my panic was quickly replaced by awe as Rylee stepped out. She was beaming in a beautiful blush gown with a white lace overlay. It had lace appliques draped off her shoulder and a removable tulle overskirt. It was perfect for the beach and *very* Rylee.

"What do you think?" she asked, holding the skirt out to the side as she spun around slowly.

I tossed my phone down and gave my best friend my full attention. "Rylee, you look breathtaking. Chance is going to cry when he sees you. I think I might cry right now." My sinuses burned as I attempted to hold back tears.

"You really think so? There are so many others to try, but as soon as I saw this one, I said to myself, *that's the one.*" She spun around to look at herself in the large floor-to-ceiling mirrors as she stepped onto the pedestal in the middle of the room.

"If you want to try the others, try them. Even if it's just for shits and giggles, hell, buy two. Get a different dress for the reception if you want. Scott's paying."

She smirked at me in the mirror and shook her head. "You're incorrigible."

"And you love me for it." I smirked back at her.

As she continued to admire the dress from all angles, I leaned forward and put my elbows on my knees, clasping my hands in my lap and clearing my throat.

"Listen, Rylee. I've been meaning to talk to you-"

"No," she interrupted.

"You don't even know what I was going to say."

"You want to move back here, and I don't want you to leave. Call me selfish, but I like having my best friend within ten minutes of me. Now, is your dress ready? I don't think I want to try anything else on because this is definitely my dress, and it's too beautiful to change into another for the reception. So, let's see you in yours," she ordered.

I blinked at her demanding tone as a stylist appeared carrying a garment bag. "I have your dress right here, Mrs. Tailor. Would you like to try it on?"

"No."

"Yes."

The stylist, I think her name was Celeste, didn't appear phased at all as Rylee and I gave conflicting answers simultaneously. "Wonderful, I'll just get this room ready for you, and you can push the button inside if you need any help."

Sighing, I got up from the couch and grabbed my flute of champagne, downing it in one gulp. "We can talk about this later."

"No, Sadie. There's nothing to talk about. Your life is in Jacksonville. You're not going to run away and hide here in the city just because you and Tyler haven't figured your shit out. I don't know why you haven't told him about the divorce yet, but this was everything you wanted. I don't understand what the hold-up is. Why are you trying to run away *now*?"

"I don't want him to get hurt because of me. At least, no more than I've already hurt him," I replied automatically, voicing my concerns for the first time out loud.

Her face softened as she walked over, mindful of the train of her dress getting caught on anything. She took my hand and peered up at me as an errant thought went through my head that I should probably wear flats if Rylee wore footless sandals for the wedding.

"Look, I know that it seems scary because Scott threatened to—" she looked around before lowering her voice, "-kill him. But he promised you Tyler would be okay. Do you really think Scott would leave you alone if this Morroni guy were that big of a problem? He's probably got guys watching you right now, as creepy as that is. But if they are watching you, they'd be watching Tyler, right? So wouldn't you both be protected, then?"

"It isn't just that, Ry. He seems happy without me. Maybe I should just let him be happy. By the time the wedding rolls around, we'll have been apart long enough to walk down the aisle together amicably. Just do me a favor and warn me if he plans on bringing a date." I dropped her hand to grab the champagne bottle out of the bucket of ice and poured myself another glass.

As I turned back to her, a sharp pain stung the side of my head as she smacked me. "Ow, Rylee, what the hell?"

"I'm gonna do worse if you keep that shit up. You two are ridiculous, and frankly, Chance and I are tired of being in the middle of it. It's like a never-ending episode of *Days of our Lives*. You both love each other, and there is absolutely nothing standing in the way of you two being together. The only obstacles you guys have to overcome are in here," she said as she shoved her pointer finger into my temple.

Swatting her hand away, I moved around her to go change. Deep down, I knew she was right, but I was afraid to put myself out there again with Tyler. I grew anxious while I slipped into my dress and wondered if he'd replied to my message.

Stepping out of the fitting room, I held my hands out and quickly spun without looking at myself in the mirror. "Does the bride approve?"

I'd picked my dress weeks ago. It was a simple satin mid-length in a dusty lavender. The straps were thin and crossed in the back, and there was ruching on one side of the waist that pulled the skirt up asymmetrically.

"Yes, I approve, but that's your *only* decision I approve of right now." Rylee sniffed with feigned snobbery. I gave her a pointed look, and a few moments later, we were both laughing.

We collapsed on the couch, shoulder to shoulder, drinking more champagne and letting the conversation drift to wedding details. The stylists were nice enough to let us spend as much time as we wanted without feeling like we needed to leave, so we finished the bottle, then went to find lunch.

As the rest of the day progressed, I continuously checked my phone to see if Tyler had replied, but he hadn't. Now and then, I'd see the three dots pop up that meant someone was in the middle of responding, but each time they disappeared as quickly as they'd appeared.

That night, sleep eluded me as I tossed and turned and tried to accept that Tyler didn't want to talk to me. I didn't tell Rylee I'd reached out, partly because I didn't want her to make a big deal out of it. I knew if she did, it would only get my hopes up, and the sting of rejection I'd been waiting for would be that much worse.

Silence was worse than rejection, though.

As the sun filtered through my room the following day, the bags and boxes I'd pulled out to move to Jacksonville remained empty, much like the Tyler-shaped void in my chest.

CHAPTER TWENTY-THREE

The din of the bar was quiet for a Saturday night. Riya had taken the weekend off to return to Vegas for a friend's birthday, so I'd stepped back into my old role as bartender. Our sales had been great lately, but tonight I wondered if there was an event going on in town I didn't know about, because there had been fewer than twenty people for the majority of the evening. If it kept up this way, I'd be closing down early.

"Wow, we're dead," Rylee's voice drifted over my shoulder, startling and causing me to jump and spin around.

"Damn, you little ninja! I didn't even hear you come in. What are you doing here? I thought Chance wasn't feeling good?" A regular at the end of the bar lifted a hand to get my attention and signaled that he wanted another beer.

"He has a man cold and is sleeping it off. I was

bored. Domino was all snuggled up with him, and I didn't want to disturb them, so I figured I'd come back here and hang out with you. We should close early tonight and go get drinks at Pascal's if you're not busy," she replied as she grabbed a new drink for the customer.

"Why would I be busy? My life is boring now that you're wifed up." I leaned against the bar top with my back to the door while she took the guy his beer.

There was a fine layer of dust on the glass shelves that held the top shelf liquor, and I realized it was time to close down and clean again. With everything that had been happening, I'd forgotten to schedule the cleaners, and since I was still in Jacksonville, it was technically still my job.

Sighing, I added it to my mental list of things I needed to do, next to arranging a block of hotel rooms for the guests attending Chance and Rylee's wedding. I also needed to call Sarah Lewis and tell her I'd decided against changing my last name, so we didn't need to worry about additional paperwork.

The divorce was finalized, and Scott had been relatively amicable during the few times we'd talked since he'd shown up on my doorstep here in Florida. Though something was still tugging at my mind about *why* he was suddenly so agreeable.

True to his word, he'd vacated the penthouse when I wanted to return to New York. For now, I'd told him we could remain sharing it because there was no need for him to leave the home we'd known for twenty years if I wasn't going to be there most of the time.

A chime rang through the air as someone opened the front door. My eyes traveled from the bottles on the shelves to the mirrored wall behind them, and my breath caught in my throat. Tyler's eyes stared back at mine through the mirror, and I inhaled sharply before turning to face him.

My mouth watered, and my body tightened instantly, as if on autopilot. The mere sight of him reminded my muscles of what they needed to do in preparation for taking him inside me–as if I could ever forget.

We stared at each other silently for a few moments before he took a step forward, and I remembered I needed to breathe. His steps were slow, and he had the hood of his ever-present zip-up pulled over his head. Neither of us said a word as he sat on the stool in front of me and leaned over the bar top.

Slowly, he reached for my hand, and the rest of the bar faded away until it was just the two of us.

"Hello, lovely lady. I'm Tyler, your future husband," he said, smooth and quiet, for my ears only.

Laughing softly as tears pricked my eyes, my hand grasped his tightly. A wave of relief flooded through me at the words he'd spoken when we first met. To continue the replay of our meet cute, I held up my left hand to show him my naked ring finger. "Well, that's good to know, Tyler. I happen to be newly single. Was thinking about adopting a puppy."

He smiled, and I nearly melted. "I love puppies," he replied. "And early morning swims. And turtles. But most of all, I love you. I'm sorry for how we left things and for taking so long to get here, but I'd like to start over."

I was around the bar and in his arms in seconds. He stood as we clutched each other tightly. I don't know how long we stayed like that before I heard Rylee suggest quietly, "Why don't you two go back to the office?"

Tyler nodded at her against my hair, and I sniffed as he pulled me to the back. My eyes connected with my friend's as we shared a smile, and I briefly wondered if this was the reason she'd shown back up tonight.

Neither of us said a word as we walked down the hall hand in hand, but as soon as the office door shut behind him, he pulled me into his arms again. "I missed you so much," he breathed against my hair.

"I missed you too. I didn't think you wanted to speak to me after you never replied to my text," I told him as I pulled back.

He let go of me and pushed his hood off his head, running a hand through his hair. "I wanted to. I almost did right away. But I just needed a little more time, Sadie."

"I know. I know I said a lot of hurtful things to

you. I hope you know I didn't mean a word of it, Tyler. Scott threatened-"

"Rylee told me. She told me everything. Just me. She didn't mention anything in front of Chance, so please don't get mad at her. She kept her promise."

Nodding, I stepped around him, crossing the room to lean against my desk. Tyler stayed where he was by the door, putting half the room between us. "So you know I did what I did to protect you."

"I *understand* why you did what you did. But I wish you had spoken to me first. I don't know what we would have done, but at least we could have figured something out together. I know with Scott, you were used to being on your own, but in a normal relationship, in *our* relationship, we're a team. We can handle whatever comes our way, as long as we do it *together*." He leaned against the door as he spoke. His words reminded me how young he was and how jaded I was regarding relationships.

But they also gave me hope.

"What are you saying? That there is still an us?" I asked, looking at the floor so I didn't have to see the potential rejection on his face.

"Yes, but I want to take things slow this time. I want to take you out on a real date and ask you all the things I normally would have. Get to know you the way I didn't even try to before. I realized I know very little about you, Sadie Tailor. And I want to know everything."

"Slow, huh? I think I'm okay with that." I leaned

back a little and put my weight on my hands, my skirt riding up as I uncrossed my legs. My heart jumped as his eyes went straight to the space between my thighs. He swallowed thickly, and his eyes darkened.

"I guess that means no sex then, right? I'm normally a five-date kind of girl before I sleep with someone." I shrugged as I effortlessly slipped back into the ease of the physical side of our connection.

He licked his lips before raising his gaze to mine. My body went tight, and my lower belly flooded with heat as he stalked toward me with a predatory gleam in his eyes.

"We can start slow tomorrow, then. Right now, I need to make you wonder why the fuck you left me in the first place."

I whimpered as he stopped before me, reaching out to grip the back of my neck. My lips parted as he tilted his head like he would kiss me, but his lips stopped, hovering just over mine.

"Tell me you're mine," he whispered, our lips touching for the briefest of moments.

"I'm yours, Tyler." I slid my hands up his chest and twisted them in his hair in an attempt to pull him down to me.

He resisted, and his grip on my neck tightened as he continued to tease me with gentle, barely-there nips. Finally, he smirked before he crushed his lips to mine. It was a hard and punishing kiss, and I loved every second of how our mouths molded together again, like they were old lovers greeting each other.

Sucking my lower lip into his mouth, he bit it harshly, causing me to suck in a breath. Then he let go of me suddenly, my mind reeling as I felt his hands push me back, and I opened my eyes to see him drop to his knees.

He pulled me to the edge of the desk and pushed my skirt up before he pulled my underwear down my legs and tossed the scrap of fabric aside. My breathing became labored as he hooked my legs over his shoulders, and my hand found the top of his head. His tongue swept up my center and circled my clit before he latched on and started to suck.

"Fuck, Tyler!" I cried out. His arduous pace didn't let up as he looked at me, and *fuck* if it wasn't one of the hottest things I'd ever seen. There was something about watching as a man devoured your most sensitive part.

There was nothing slow about the way Tyler ate me out. It was like he was trying to win a fucking race, and my body was thrumming with pleasure so intense that I felt dizzy. "Tyler, I'm not going to last."

My hand tightened in his hair, pulling him closer to me as I ground against his face. His hands gripped my thighs so tight that it bordered on pain. I cried out as I came, and Tyler brought two fingers to my opening to coat them in my release as he slowed his ministrations on my clit.

My body spasmed as he lay his tongue flat

against me and lapped up what was left, before he stuck his fingers in his mouth and licked them clean. He reached for my skirt, kissing the inside of my thigh before he pulled it down and whispered, "Good girl."

"Your turn." I reached for him, but he grabbed my wrists and stopped me from touching him.

"If you touch me now, I'll lock you up, and we won't leave the bed for a week. This time it's going to be about more than fucking, Sadie. I wanna do this right. But trust me, that was just as much for me as it was for you."

He stood, his erection a hard outline against his jeans, and I licked my lips as I reached for my underwear that he'd grabbed, but he shook his head and stuffed them in his pants pocket. "Oh no. I'm definitely going home to jerk off into these."

We shared a laugh as he kissed me lightly. "How about we go on that first date tomorrow? Dinner? I'll pick you up at seven?"

My arms wound around his neck as I nodded. "Sounds good, Pup. And for you, I'll make an exception."

"An exception?" he asked with a raised brow.

Pulling him down, I smirked against his lips before replying, "For you, I'll be a one-date kind of girl."

The sky was lit up with vibrant pinks and purples against the blues and oranges of the sunset, creating a perfect backdrop for Chance and Rylee's wedding. An arch made of wood was draped in light pink chiffon, with clusters of white and pink roses and greenery winding around it. The aisle was covered in pink rose petals, and large lanterns glowed at the end of each row of chairs that were filled with guests waiting for the ceremony to start.

One year ago today, Tyler and Chance walked into Sugar and Scotch and turned mine and Rylee's world upside down.

One year ago, Chance had told Rylee that on this day, they might be standing right here, where they had their first date, saying their wedding vows.

Part of me wanted to gag at how cute they were.

My eyes drifted to the two men standing under the arch where Tyler was watching me and blew a kiss my way, causing a smile to light up my face. Okay, it wasn't as if we were any better.

For wanting to take things slow, things between us had progressed quickly. I'd sold my condo and moved in with him. My only request had been allowing me to turn the second living room into a walk-in closet, to which he'd readily agreed. Ashlee made disparaging comments about it every time she was in town, but I kept reminding her I could have turned the guest room into my closet instead, and she usually shut up.

She and I are working to have some sort of relationship, for Tyler's sake.

I was also now a proud co-parent of a four-month-old golden retriever rescue that we named Donatello. He was currently tormenting Domino at Chance and Rylee's with a pet sitter. Gary was not pleased.

Turning from the beach, I walked through the backyard of the house that belonged to Chance and Tyler's clients. They were out of town and told the guys they'd be more than happy to lend them the place for everyone to get ready.

Knocking on the door of the master bedroom, I called out, "Ry, you almost ready?"

"Yes! Get in here," she called back.

Opening the door, I smiled at the scene before me. Rylee's mother and Lynette were fussing over her train, while her sister lounged on the bed with a glass of champagne. From the moment I met Rysta, I hadn't liked her. She was bratty and tried to make Rylee feel inadequate at every possible turn, and the way she and Chance's dad, Devon, carried on made me want to throw up.

Rylee and I were fairly certain they were sharing a hotel room.

"Okay, everyone. Let's take our places before we lose the sun," I told them.

Rylee and I waited until everyone shuffled out before I picked up her train and helped her down the stairs. "Ready to become Mrs. Rylee Birchem?"

She laughed as we made our way through the house, to the sliding glass doors that led to the back-yard. "I'm *so* ready. This is so crazy. Can you believe I'm getting married?"

"Yes, absolutely I can. You two deserve this." I tweaked a strand of her hair as it spilled over her shoulder and secured it back behind the clip that held it up. Rylee's dad appeared and smiled at me as I stepped back and looked her over to ensure every-thing was in place.

"Showtime," I told her, as a rendition of "Can't Help Falling in Love" started to play softly.

Stepping out through the doors, I took Tyler's arm as he held it out for me. "You look fucking beau-tiful. Have I told you that tonight?" he whispered.

Leaning over, I kissed him softly. "You tell me that every hour of every day. You look quite hand-some yourself."

His suit was a dove gray, while his tie was a deep

navy that matched Chance's suit. It was a color I hadn't seen him wear, and it did things to my insides that left me feeling hot, despite the slight breeze.

We stared at each other, his eyes darkening as my breath quickened. Someone cleared their throat, and it pulled me from the moment as I remembered it was time for us to make our way down the aisle.

Tyler chuckled as we started to walk. Once we got close to the end, just before we were about to go to our opposite sides of the arch, he leaned over and whispered, "One of these days, this will be us."

His words shocked me as I took my place and turned to watch as Rylee appeared. Her soft pink smile was wide as her eyes locked with Chance. I snuck a glance at him, and just as I had predicted, he was struggling not to cry.

Mine and Tyler's eyes remained on each other throughout the ceremony, and I wondered about his comment. I wasn't even sure I wanted to get married again, and I hadn't realized that it was even something he'd been thinking about.

As George pronounced Chance and Rylee husband and wife, Tyler mouthed *I love you* and warmth spread in my chest as I mouthed back, *I love you, too.*

Tyler

Sugar and Scotch was packed as the reception lasted well into the night. I'd slipped away to call the pet sitter, and when I came back inside, Chance was getting up on stage to announce that he'd prepared a little something for Rylee.

The opening chords of ABBA's "Waterloo" started, and I rolled my eyes with a grin as I searched for Sadie in the crowd. We'd heard enough of this song. Chance had been practicing it in my home gym for the last month.

My eyes landed on her just as she disappeared through the doors that led to the kitchen, and I made my way through the people laughing and cheering on Chance as he sang to Rylee, who sat on a chair in the middle of the dance floor.

Sadie spun around with a cupcake in her hand as I came through the doors, licking chocolate ganache off her finger. My cock stirred at the sight, and I let out a low groan as I walked toward her.

"As much as I love those two, I can't stomach that song anymore. Plus I was hungry." She scooped a dollop of frosting onto her finger and held it out for me to taste as she laughed.

Her finger retreated as I came closer, until I had her pressed against the counter by my hips, and she wiped the frosting down her neck. My hands found her waist as my head dipped to lick up the mess she'd made. She made a noise low in her throat, and I pressed my erection into her, pulling my head back.

"I'm hungry for something else," I murmured against her skin.

"Like this?" she asked, wiping another smear of frosting across the top of her left breast.

She arched her back as I ripped the strap of her dress down and licked the trail of chocolate off her skin, before I took her nipple in my mouth and flicked it with my tongue. Letting go of it with a pop, I reached up to massage it as I watched her get more frosting from the cupcake.

Sadie started to lower her hand between us, and mine shot out so quickly to grab it that she sucked in a surprised breath. "Don't you dare," I warned.

"Why not?" she asked in a breathy whisper.

My thumb flicked her nipple once more before I slid my hand down beneath her skirt. She let out a whimper as I reached under the band of her underwear and swiped two fingers up her center.

Lifting my hand between us, I brought my fingers to my lips as I pushed her chocolate-coated finger to hers. "Because I fucking love the way you taste, just the way you are."

Sucking my fingers clean, I watched as she did the same before I started to undo the belt of my pants. "I need to be inside you."

Sadie set the cupcake down, lifted her skirt, and pulled her thong to the side as I freed my cock and sank into her. She rested her weight on the table behind her with one hand, and the other found my shoulder as I hitched one of her legs around my hip and started to thrust into her.

"We should have gone to the office," she groaned

as I picked up my pace and reached between us to rub my thumb against her clit.

"Let someone walk in on us. I don't care. The only thing I care about right now is you coming on my cock," I told her huskily.

She leaned back further, and the new position gave me deeper access as I bottomed out inside her. She rolled her hips against me as I fucked her faster, and we both came with a loud cry as the crowd outside cheered as Chance ended his performance.

I rested my sweaty forehead on hers and kissed her lightly. "I want to fuck you every day for the rest of our lives."

My cock still pulsed inside her as she replied, "That's the plan, Pup."

The bar was down to a few remaining guests as Sadie and I slowly swayed to the last song of the night. Chance and Rylee had left a little while ago for their night in the honeymoon suite her parents had gifted them. Ashlee had gone to relieve the pet sitter and planned to stay at Chance and Rylee's for the night.

"So, I've been thinking," I said quietly against her hair.

"Oh yeah? What about?" she asked.

Pulling back, I swallowed nervously. "About what's next for us."

She grinned before leaning in to kiss me lightly. "And what are you thinking is next, Pup?"

Stepping back, I cleared my throat as I let her go to reach into the inside pocket of my suit jacket. Her eyes widened at the navy box I pulled out, and her hands flew up to cover her mouth. "Oh my God, Tyler."

"I just want to preface this by saying this doesn't have to mean what you think it means if you don't want it to. I can understand if getting married again isn't something you want to do. But if it's not, I'd like you to at least consider wearing it so that no man ever gets confused about your relationship status." My palms started to sweat as I opened the Harry Winston box.

Sadie and I had discussed the extent of my wealth, and she'd made it very clear she didn't expect me to treat her the way Scott had. The ring she was currently looking at was much smaller than the one he'd given her, but the sales lady at Harry Winston had told me that Sadie had been eyeing the canary diamond ring for as long as she could remember, and my girl deserved to sparkle.

"I didn't want to cause a scene or put you on the spot. If you don't want to answer me now—"

"Yes," she interrupted.

"-then that's okay, I can wait. Wait. Yes?" Relief shot through me, and a giant weight felt like it lifted off my shoulders as Sadie's radiant smile lit up her face.

"Yes, Tyler. Whatever you're asking, the answer is yes. And you didn't have to get me a fancy ring. I would have said yes to an empty box." She threw her arms around my neck, and I squeezed her tightly.

"My answer is yes to any question you ever ask me for the rest of our lives. I love you so much," she whispered in my ear.

I pulled back to slide the ring onto her finger as I cocked an eyebrow. "*Any* question?"

She admired the twisted platinum band with pave diamonds surrounding the oval-shaped, two-and-a-half-carat canary diamond as she replied confidently, "Yes. Any question."

"Okay, well, in that case, I was thinking about getting some pet turtles," I joked, pulling her back into my arms.

Sadie laughed and kissed me. "Let's talk about it after the *actual* pup grows up. Deal?"

"I was kidding, but if you're up for it, then deal. The only thing I need to be happy is you, Wifey. Damn, that's gonna be a real title now, isn't it?"

"It sure as hell is, Pup."

Scott, Carmela, Jackson, and Ginny will be back.

Flip the page for a look into New York's hottest new club coming to you next year

Have you ever had a desire so dark you wouldn't dare speak it out loud? You've buried it so deep in the depths of your soul, but it's always there.

Wanting.

Waiting for the moment you set it free.

Our Temptangels will awaken your deepest hunger.

Here, you can feast until you're satiated.

Here, you can be whoever you want and do whatever you wish—with consent, of course.

Whether a woman or a man, or both if you prefer, your pleasure is their delight. Take a mask, pick your angel, and let your dreams take flight.

Welcome to Désirer

AFTERWORD

Oh goodness! I am equal parts sad and thrilled to see this series come to an end. Sad, because of course we have to say goodbye to our golden retriever and pup. Thrilled, because I get to start working on the next series.

I was a quarter of the way through this book when the idea hit me to tie it in with another idea I've had for a while. I had to pause to see if I could make all the pieces fit, but when it came together in my outline, I was overjoyed. From there, Jackson and Ginny were born. Carmela decided she'd make an appearance, and the senator. There is so much foreshadowing for what's to come and I can't wait to see reader's reactions and theories on why Scott all of a sudden decided to let Sadie go.

As much as he needed to be a villain, he kept yelling at me that he wasn't THAT horrible. But I guess you will have to wait and see for yourselves.

For those of you who are still confused as to how this duet ties in with Where the Flowers Bloom, Ashlee—Tyler's sister, is Daphne's salon manager. She's mentioned only one time in WTFB but Daphne was mentioned in this book with a little sneak peek at how her life is going.

And of course, there's Jess and Sean. Those two are always a blast to write.

Don't worry, you'll get to see the gang back together at Bill and Birdie's wedding in August! Make sure to subscribe to my newsletter so you don't miss out on their bonus chapter!

And make sure to check out the print version of this book for a sneak peek into the new series that's coming next year.

ACKNOWLEDGMENTS

As always, I want to thank my incredible husband for putting up with all of my mood swings during writing. And for enduring questions from our friends about getting a divorce due to my storytime shenanigans on TikTok. We are happily married everyone.

A.R. Rose and Jessica Hoffa, you two are my absolute backbone and my bestest writing friends. I don't know what I would do without either of you. Thank you for talking me through all of my mental breakdowns during writing. And special thanks to A.R. for teaching me how to do basically anything and everything in Canva to plug into Vellum. And also pretty much everything writing in general.

Cassie Merritt, my PA, thanks for taking me on and putting up with my nonsense.

To my editor, Virginia Carey, you're so amazing!

Thank you to the readers who reach out. To all of you who support us indie authors. To those of you who have stuck with me since the beginning. It's only been a couple of months, but we have a long way to go! Your continued support and kind words lift me up and make me want to keep writing.

XO

D.L. Darby lives with her husband, dog, and cat, in Anchorage, Alaska. When she's not at her salon or writing, she's usually outside hiking (when the weather allows it), snuggled up with her animals reading a book, or filming a ridiculous amount of TikTok's for the upcoming month.

You can join her reader group, D.L. Darby's Darlings on Facebook. Or follow her on Instagram and/or TikTok @d.l.darby_author

www.dldarbyauthor.com

9 798986 997322